BAYOU CRESTING

BAYOU CRESTING

The Wanting Women of Huet Pointe

a novel-in-stories by

Jodie Cain Smith

CROWSNEST BOOKS

Crowsnest Books
www.crowsnestbooks.com

Distributed by the University of Toronto Press

Cataloguing data available from Library and Archives Canada.

ISBN: 978-0921332-76-3 (paperback)

ISBN: 978-0921332-77-0 (eBook)

This is a work of fiction. Names, characters, places, events, and incidents are either the products of the author's imagination or used in a fictitious manner. Any resemblance to actual persons, living or dead, or actual events is purely coincidental.

Typeset in American Typewriter, designed by Joel Kaden and Tony Stan, and Adobe Caslon, designed by Carol Twombly.

Printed and bound in Canada

FOR THOSE WHO EXPECT MORE

Contents

Acknowledgements

Writing is often a solitary task with hours spent in isolation with a keyboard and the nagging of characters, plot points, and scenic elements, each demanding their due on the page. Transforming a manuscript into a novel, however, is not a solitary task. *Bayou Cresting: The Wanting Women of Huet Pointe* certainly was not. A slew of people helped me birth this book baby.

Lewis Slawsky and Alex Wall of Crowsnest Books proved to be the kind of publishers all writers wish to find. I am so fortunate that they took a chance on an unknown, were excited about the work and let my crazy women live on the page exactly how I wanted. Thank you, Lewis and Alex, for trusting my voice and for bringing my quirky vision to fruition.

The women of Huet Pointe first arrived in my mind's eye years ago with a flash fiction challenge between two friends. Thank you, Kasie, for challenging me to attempt the first short story of Huet Pointe, and the first short story I ever wrote. After Kasie prompted the start, my friend and walking buddy Julianne picked up the proverbial baton. Thank you, Julianne, for pounding the pavement with me as we brainstormed Huet Pointe society and pondered the question, "Just what does a woman have to do to achieve her ambition in this world?"

As far as I am concerned, I won the lottery of critique groups. Betsy, Frank, Jim, Linda, and Mike, you improved my work so much with your kind and thoughtful critiques. Where would Huet Pointe and all its women be without our meetings and your encouragement? I'd rather not imagine my writing life without this group, as I am spoiled beyond recovery by each of you, so I will simply thank you and get to work on my pages for our next meeting.

Thank you, Mama and Daddy, the people who taught me to stand up for myself and what I want and that achievement requires effort, so I better be willing to do the hard work. Mama, you are a force of womanhood. Daddy, you're the father every woman needs.

To my guys, Jay and Bay, how boring my life would be without you two in it. Jay, thank you for giving me the space to write and for reminding me that I am "Trying to do something really hard. It's going to take time." Your support of my big dream means everything to me. And, my sweet Bay, you give me so much love and joy every day. I hope I make you proud and that you will always smile when you say, "My mama writes stories."

Finally, to my readers, thank you so much for exploring Huet Pointe and my eclectic gaggle of women in these pages. I hope you enjoy your visit.

Part One: Summer

Mamba Loo

"You ain't no different from all us. Here in Huet Pointe, we nothing to them. So, you got to learn. You got to become nothing. You got to empty yourself of all that pain and fill it up with what they don't know." Mamba Loo's voice rose well over the cicadas' song. They'd walked undetected through the sugarcane field, the round, solid Voodoo priestess and her pupil, Sabine. The green stalks had done well to conceal their midnight excursion with the bright moon lighting their way. But, now, in the tree line, the plentiful pines blocked the light.

"What I got to do is sleep." Sabine tracked behind Mamba Loo down the narrow, rugged path, her right foot wrinkling in the damp sole of her boot. Her calves tightened as the ground sloped toward the creek. She had planned to stitch the hole in her boot that very night, but Mamba Loo had other plans for the recent girl-turned-woman. And, none of their social circle turned away Mamba Loo. Now, hours later and the hole ripping wider with every step, she marched behind her teacher. Resistance only prolonged Mamba Loo's teaching.

"Mamba's gonna learn you all you need." As she gulped down a breath needed for teaching and walking and talking, the older woman paused and raised one arm. The sugarcane stalk she'd been chewing waved against the breeze then fell still, as if on command. Mamba Loo, now a black statue in dingy white skirt and blouse, examined the sweet shoot. Her breath silenced and muscles tensed as she held the stalk high in the air, silently begging it to move. "Do you hear them?" the woman whispered.

Sabine nearly bumped into Mamba in the darkness of the path; their mud-stained skirts brushing against each other's. "Sleep, Mamba. I need sleep. And I planned to stitch up this hole in my boot tonight. They had finally dried out enough to – "

"Quiet, child!" Mamba Loo glared at Sabine. "Can't you feel 'em? They's all around us now." Her bare feet planted in the muck like roots of a mighty oak. She craned her neck and peered into the dark forest.

Sabine froze, familiar with the stories of Mamba Loo's ability to feel spirits and of the spirits' proclivity to awaken at midnight. The tree line began to whisper. The cries of untethered, discontented souls escaped the trees and fell in Sabine's diminutive ears. At least that's what the chill rising in her spine indicated.

"Mamba," Sabine pleaded, no louder than the muttering of a mouse.

"Hush, child. Listen to them."

Mamba Loo's intuition had kept her alive despite the efforts of many a foreman, master, and mistress across the South. If her memory was correct, she'd served in four households. The first was an impressive Georgian home with sprawling porches and columns climbing two stories toward the Charleston sky.

Walking along the Battery, her mother had told Mamba of her gift. "Millie," her mother said, speaking in lyrical but broken English decades before Mamba Loo earned the title of a Voodoo priestess and spiritual guide to all she counseled. "You chosen. You's chosen to be wise and knowing. And I know. Trust Mama. You see, child, most babies break their sacs as they fightin' and kickin' to come out. But not you, my sweet. You wise then even, just a teeny thing, but wise. You knew to keep your sac on as long as you could 'cause you already know what's out here in the world. That caul done taught you to stay protected as long you can."

"Protected from what? Who?" Young Millie rubbed her thumb against her mother's hand, finding comfort in the dry, rough skin.

"They's spirits in the world. Some good, some bad. Some them devils jump in an unsuspecting vessel and grab holt. Most us cain't feel 'em, cain't hear 'em, but you will. That's what that caul done give you. Soon as Lou-Lou pulled you out of me, I saw it. You still swimming in that sac, your tiny fingers covering your face like you not ready to see what you gotta see, to hear what you gotta hear. But it's time for you to see and hear and listen."

From then on, Millie listened to the trees at night. They told her when change approached, good or bad. The trees told her to run to her mama's bedside as the fever overtook her body. They told her to let her mama go, that she'd suffered enough. The trees told her to avoid the master and all four of his sons. And the trees told her when to leave Charleston.

As soon as she reached maturity at thirteen, the trees reported to her the envious nature of her Charleston mistress, enflamed by the wandering eyes of her master. A man in Atlanta bought Mamba the very next week.

Her second home, a grand Gothic Revival at the end of a long, gravel driveway lined with oak trees, proved more treacherous with every whisper from the trees. Beware the foreman. Beware the head butler. *Accept the whip.* For her refusal of the butler, she got the whip. For her failed attempts at refusing the foreman, the whip left scars no salve could soften. Soon after, she was traded to a family in Mobile, after the baleful Scotsman with a slick head and sour pits grew bored with the chase.

In Mobile, the spirits fell silent. For months they remained mute, waiting until she had given herself over to her master. She'd judged him to be kind enough, although still ruled by his immoral urges. She'd allowed him to come into her bedroom night after night. With barely enough space for her cot, chair, and wardrobe, she spread her legs as he lowered himself onto her, his blue eyes shut as if not looking at her lessened his sin.

Months passed before the trees awoke one January evening, screaming with fright for her and the infant tucked next to her—blue eyes alight as if he too heard the sound. Their screams crashed through the tiny window one minute before her bedroom door burst open. Her mistress ripped her from her bed, digging her nails into Millie's flesh. The mistress cursed the bastard child and the whore who bore him. *Abomination! Sin incarnate!* Millie wiped the spittle from her cheek. For that, the mistress rewarded Millie with a slap so hard the baby nearly sprang from her arms.

With only the baby boy and the nightgown she wore, she was banished, sold to the Durand Plantation in Huet Pointe for pennies on the dollar. Over the next several hours, Millie feared the frigid dawn ride in the open wagon would kill her. Her naked toes burned as she tried to cover as much of her skin as possible with the thin cotton gown. With her right arm shackled to the wagon, she held the baby to her breast with her left arm. Within a few hours, her left arm began to spasm. A few hours more and the spasms stopped, replaced by numbness more troubling than the twitching and wringing.

The man shackled next to her, a field hand from a plantation an hour west of Mobile, offered to hold the baby for her. Millie considered his offer, but refused. What if he tossed the crying baby from the wagon? Nothing, not even a baby tossed into the brush, would stop the two drivers, paid only half up front.

At last, with shriveled tongue and her stomach twisted from hunger, the wagon reached the bayou crossing. As she rocked back and forth on the small barge, the middle-aged porter ogled her barely covered breasts. Millie lacked the strength to turn her back to him or even purse her cracked lips.

Although her vision blurred from exhaustion, she marveled at the afternoon sun dancing off the brown water. The ripples smiled at her. She lacked the strength to return the smile, but she made a deal with the spirits of Huet Pointe. If they agreed to keep her safe there with the shimmering water and trees taller than she'd ever seen, she'd never give herself over to another man again. She promised to devote herself to her son and to the trees, her Iwa manifestation. So, she perfected the ways of her mother and grandmother and all the women who went before her to guide the lost and burdened and frightened.

To do this, she made herself undesirable. She chopped at her hair so that without a tignon to cover her head, she looked as if a rat had crawled from the swamp and chewed her hair away. She snuck extra pats of butter, biscuits, and whatever else she could smuggle from the kitchen. With her teeth and tongue, she cleaned the chicken bones and dinner plates of her new charges. After one year, she glanced at her reflection in her new mistress's bedroom and smiled, pleased with the plump, aging woman she'd become.

After two years in Huet Pointe, she'd earned the title Mamba. She chose Loo to honor the woman who'd washed the caul from her coffee-colored skin, dark eyes, and ears, now open to hear the spirits as few on Earth could.

For the first time in her life, Mamba felt secure. She'd made herself indispensable in Huet Pointe for her wide range of home remedies, miracle salves, affective conjures, and ability to calm any crying baby or toddler simply by resting them upon her substantial bosom. To the white women of Huet Pointe, she became essential, although not a one dared say so out loud.

"You hear 'em, Sabine? You ears open?" Mamba Loo asked, arms wide and raised to the heavens.

"I'm...I'm..." Sabine whispered, trembling, "What happens if they breathe on you?"

"You feel that on the back of yo' neck, don' cha?" Mamba Loo turned and grinned at Sabine with large, white teeth framed in thick, purple lips. "That's good. Means they want you to know they're here with you. But don't brush up any of 'em by accident.

They don't like it when you's so wrapped up in you own you forget they there."

Sabine stood as still as she could, petrified to bump a spirit.

"You see that!" whisper-yelled Mamba Loo, pointing down the path before them. "A rabbit! Blessed be! We's on the right path now. He done showed us." Mamba Loo tossed the sugarcane stalk aside and picked up her skirts. Light-footed down the path, she moved as if her feet and legs were decades younger than the folds on her neck. "Hurry, Sabine. We got's to get that toad!"

"Toad? I thought we were listening to spirits!" Sabine tried to keep up with Mamba, the bottom of her boot spitting water and mud with every quick step.

"I did! We listened good so they give me a sign," Mamba yelled, still running. "That rabbit is the spirits telling me to keep going. That what I been needin'..." Mamba stopped with such abruptness she nearly fell forward into the shallows of the creek. She reached down, plunging one hand into the muck. Turning, she held her hand out to Sabine. "This! This! I finally got it!" The toad, probably from being squeezed in Mamba's mighty grasp, croaked and blinked his wet eyes at Sabine as if begging for help.

Nearly the size of Mamba's forearm and covered in pearl shaped bumps, the toad croaked slow and loud. Faint stripes extended from his nose, over his head and bulbous neck, and down to the rounded tip of his butt.

"I ain't never seen one this perfect before."

"I didn't know toads could get that big," Sabine said, backing away from her teacher. "What is it for?" Mamba Loo had already taught Sabine to never take from nature what you will not use, so she knew Mamba Loo had a plan for the frightened creature.

"My momma when I's young told me something you need to know. Not all the spirits out here is good. Some is bad. Real bad. Some jump into a living body and make them do the devil's commands. Now, once that happens, they's only a couple things you can do to save 'em. Well, I know somebody who done the devil's biddin'."

"And the toad will help the person?"

"No. The toad will help me." Mamba Loo pulled a dishtowel from her apron pocket and wrapped it around the frog, trapping it in her pocket. She marched the entire way back to the tree line, through the sugarcane field, and to her shack on the edge of the Durand Plantation without a single word to Sabine, at least none for Sabine to comprehend. Mamba muttered about bits of red cloth, needles, and whether or not it was too late in the evening to roast something.

Later that evening, after careful preparations and an hour of fervent prayer, Mamba Loo snuck out of her shack for the second time that evening. At the neighboring plantation, she burst from the tree line, displaying the same quickness through the shadows she had near the creek. Breathing hard and sweating, she stopped just in front of the grand, antebellum home. She slipped her hand into her pocket and retrieved a linen sack. With care, she lifted the conjured article out of its temporary tomb. The large toad, dead, its flesh crisped on the spit, had red strips of fabric tied to each leg. Silver needles pierced the fabric. Mamba Loo laid the curse on the doorstep and then glanced toward heaven. "It won't be long now," she said and dashed back into the trees, hot breath on her neck as she hurried home.

Sabine 1

FOR THOSE WHO HAVE LITTLE, each possession is valued. Some are priceless.

Sabine headed straight to her shack as soon as she arrived back to the Lawry parcel. The main house was vast but lacking in good taste or finery. She shuddered at the thought of her mistress lurking in dark corners, drunk and waiting to extol her demons. From the far side of the property, Sabine heard hooting and hollering, no doubt the result of passing a jug of whiskey up and down the planked porch of the bunkhouse. She wanted no part of the others employed by Ray Don and Marguerite Lawry or their carousing. As soon as she pushed the latch down on the inside of her door, she pulled off her damp boots and stockings. Her toes suggested dead minnows, pale and bloated; skin so drenched it threatened to rip.

Sabine's quarters, "the cabin I provide you," Miz Lawry told her day after day, was nothing more than a shed, bare-walled except for the jagged splinters that snagged her blouses and catch on her skirts whenever she walked through the narrow doorway. In the corner, a messily mortared hearth and fireplace stood, the flue always open, so that Sabine would have to prop a board and rocks against the opening when it was too warm to sleep without a fire burning. On nights too warm to sleep without a fire burning, Sabine blocked the fireplace opening with boards and rocks. If not, the rats and possums and raccoons saw her mattress and warm body as a comfortable place to sleep.

Sabine had few possessions to call her own and kept them well hidden within the walls, within the ticking of her bed, or beneath uneven floorboards, for which she thanked the Lord on High every morning that she had boards to set her feet upon rather than only dirt and mud. A hand-embroidered tignon given to her by a nun at Our Lady of Sorrow was tucked between the mattress cover and stuffing, folded thin so not to draw attention. The rosary presented to her on the day she completed her grammar school education and boarded passage to Huet Pointe fit perfectly behind a knot on the wall left of her slim bed. She'd wedged the charcoal pencil and paper she took from the Lawry main house in the crease between the fireplace and wall. That pencil and paper gave her hope but reminded her of an inclination to sin. *Thou shalt not steal.*

Sabine held one possession more precious than all the rest. If pressed, Sabine would surrender all her possessions to keep this one. That night in her shack, alone with barely any light, she pulled a folded piece of paper from a quarter-inch space below the foot-wide windowsill.

She glanced at the paper, in awe that years of unfolding and folding, rubbing it against her cheek, inhaling, longing for the scent washed out by air and time, had not caused the paper to disintegrate—tiny pieces of decomposed paper falling to the ground like the snow. Or, rather, what she assumed snow looked like.

With the paper in hand, she stood and peered through the window. If surprised by a midnight visitor from the main house, she didn't know if he'd burn the page, or worse, read it, stealing the words that were hers and hers alone.

Standing at the window, her mind slipped to Mamba Loo and her talk of spirits in the trees. "You must learn to listen," Mamba Loo had told her. "Listen!"

How badly Sabine wanted to yell at her mentor and friend, "Stop! The spirit I need won't ever speak to me, not in your way.

The spirit I need, I want, is not in your trees." Sabine cupped her hand over her mouth to stifle the rage that resided just below her caramel skin.

With a deep breath, she sat on her bed and unfolded the paper. She leaned back, curled on her side and read herself to sleep.

"My Dearest Sabine," the letter began. "How can a heart be so big and yet so fragile? This is the wonder I live.

"I don't know when my heart began to grow. Was it your first kick? Your first hiccup? Did it explode in size that precious moment you were first put in my arms? Still, it is big and grows bigger with every kiss.

"The mighty are strong. Prèt tells me every Sunday morning; although he cannot see me from my mandated seat, rear left, partially blocked view, a bench with no back for resting. Prèt says I should be strong. Strong against sin, against temptation, and I am. My heart is mighty, but I fear at any moment it will break apart until only shards remain. This I know will come to be.

"The others laugh at me as a fool. They say I dote on you too much, and my adoration will make you weak. They say a spoilt child is a fool like her mama. Maybe I am a fool, but the only way to prevent my heart from fragmenting is to kiss your cheeks one hundred, one thousand times a day. For every time you reach for me, wrap your tiny finger around mine, I ache. Kissing your soft cheek is my only reprieve from the pain my love for you has caused. Why should I not seek comfort from the ache? You, my angel, are the only comfort this world has for me.

"But as weak as I am, you are strong. Your tiny hand grips mine with the strength of an entire brood. You squeeze with all your might but your eyes sparkle as if to say, 'I can find more, Mama.' Yes, you will grow even stronger, if I allow you.

"You, my sweet girl, my beautiful lamb, were strong before you came into the world. When that man rose up, towered over me in anger, I felt you ready yourself. Every time he punched me, kicked me, you punched back. In my belly you fought against the cruelty surrounding you, and your strength gave me strength. Know this, my love, just as you yelled full and proud with your first breath, you will live full and proud.

"The man that seeded you tried to destroy you, but you defied his hatred of you. So, do not wonder if you had a papa. Do not waste moments staring into the pale face of every man you meet. Do not consider for a minute that any one of those devils share your blood, for you do not need them. Your blood is your own.

"Even now, as I write this on stolen paper with stolen quill and stolen ink, I hear the others whisper. They know my sins and think of you as sin incarnate. Yes, I allowed him. I obeyed without a fight. I threw no punches of my own, although my fists were always clenched. And one of them, one of the heartless ones who share my quarters will surely reveal me to him. Reveal to that hateful man all my transgressions. I will accept the whip, the lashes that will come, for what I do will give you life.

"They laugh at me for learning to read, to write, for accepting the one kindness ever offered me. They mock me as uppity and spit on my dress as I leave our quarters for the main house before dawn. They plot against me as I bathe you, feed you, sing to you. I pray they be the only ones in your life to ever call you half-breed. May no one ever call you slave. 'Why,' they ask while they laugh at me, while they plot against me, 'Why she dote over that half breed? She ignant to think her anything but a slave.'

"No, my sweet Sabine, you will not be a slave. You will be free. And with your freedom, you will live full and proud as your mama never will.

"My mighty heart will shatter as the deed is done. As I turn from you, I know you will not cry for there is no room in your spirit for tears. You will expect me to return as I always do, but I won't. As much as my breaking heart will drive me to my knees with enough agony to kill a hundred men, as much as I want to forever kiss your cheeks, I cannot return to you. You need to be free of this life. Freedom from these chains means you must be free of me. I cannot bind you to this life just to bind you to me.

"I will say a prayer each night for you, Sabine. I will pray that the Sisters of St. Michael's will love you as I love you. May they dote over you and kiss your cheeks so that you never have to wonder if you are loved. May they teach you to use your strength and to grow your strength of mind and spirit. I pray they will save this letter for you and present it to you when you begin to wonder of your mama. Above all, I pray you may know I do this for the mighty love that has filled my heart so much that it may burst with every breath.

"Once you are free, the only torture I will feel is your absence. I fear I will never escape that torture, but I will sleep knowing you will live without the scar of your beginning.

"Now, sleep, sweet Sabine, in Mama's arms. Tonight will be our last."

Maggie

WIND BLEW THROUGH the large open windows and kitchen door. This wasn't the cool breeze of fall carrying bits of browned leaves or spring wind with its yellow dusting. This was summer wind; one that caught fire over the plains then joined forces with the humidity of the coast. It carried with it red dirt from the one road leading in and out of the Lawry homestead.

The wind swirled in Maggie's kitchen, wrapping around her face like wet smoke churning inches from a flame. As a toddler incessantly pounds a tiny, wooden mallet against a table, relishing the knock-knock-knock sound, the wind blew, loosing the same strand of hair from her messy chignon so that it whipped her face and clung to the corner of her mouth again and again. The wind seemed to delight in its torture and distracted her from the flutter in her belly.

"Damn it!" She swept hard against her face, capturing the stray hairs and forcing them back into the brunette thicket at the base of her head.

"Language, Marguerite," her mother offered. The criticism pricked at Maggie's ears – a high-pitched sparrow-like noise as forceful as a mouse. "You know better, pet. And, here. Before you get peels in your hair." Josephine Alpuente offered a rag to her daughter, the one Alpuente child to survive both childbirth and the swamp.

"Mama, my hands are cleaner than this thing." Maggie tossed the rag on the floor and kicked it behind her with the heel of her boot. She watched it billow as if the wind might catch it and slap her with the stained linen. As quickly as it rose, though, it fell back to the floor and slid to the wall. She snapped her head back around to the table and her gaze fell again to three large bowls – one with whole, raw shrimp, one with broken, spindly legs and torn shells, and one with translucent, naked shrimp, perfectly peeled and deveined.

Maggie's mother, an Acadian beauty with steel blue eyes and hair so chocolate it begged to be licked, tried to make conversation, but her English was clumsy at best. Instead of helping her mother fill the hot hours with chatter, Maggie refused. She found the prattling of women as baleful as the summer wind. She didn't care how much her dear mother wished to peck and prickle about the goings-on of the bayou: A recently freed man of color hit by the new train proving the cruelty of God, the new priest, although he'd been in Huet Pointe for over a year, with his fetching jawline, bronze skin, and rolling R's. Maggie's mind was elsewhere.

"Let me help you, mon chéri," Josephine said, bumping gently against Maggie. If not for the layers of skirts and petticoats and pantaloons, they stood hip-to-hip. Using her apron, Josephine wiped flour from her hands and plucked a shrimp from the first bowl.

Maggie stared at her mother's hands. The southern sun and the decades of laundry, gardening, and cooking had tarnished her once porcelain skin as it ran over dainty knuckles, down her thin fingers to trim, petite nails. "Perhaps if I had hands like yours…"

"No, no, chéri ," Josephine said and bumped her hip against Maggie's again. "You fine with shrimp."

"I'm not talking about shrimp," Maggie answered and looked through the window. As she peered beyond the tall sycamore and river birch lining Huet Creek, a shallow rill that led to a dense swamp before the thick water dumped into the bayou, she searched for the men, knowing it was far too early for anyone to return, victorious or otherwise. Still, she strained to see through the Spanish moss and new foliage cluttering the trees.

The blood red tignon artfully wrapped about her housemaid's head interrupted Maggie's staring. Sabine glanced through the window from the porch, meeting Maggie's glare before passing. A hint of a smile crossed Maggie's face as the mouse of a girl scurried away.

"What, then?" her mother asked, looking not at Maggie but at a shrimp before twisting its head off and removing every last leg from the morsel. "Tell Mama troubles."

Had it been anyone else in the world, especially any of the perky church-belles within twenty miles of Huet's Point, Maggie would turn to the twittering bird and say, seething, ready to sink her talons into soft, pink flesh, "My hands were not made for women's work. Perhaps if my fingers were lovely and my nails clean and knuckles delicate, I could stomach the heat and wind and Godforsaken monotony of this kitchen." She couldn't, however, bring herself to raise her voice to her mother or be as vicious as her nature begged. The meadowlark might drop dead on the floor. Maggie wanted Josephine to be silent, not die.

No, her hands were not her mother's; they were her father's. As she picked up the paring knife and sliced the shrimp's back, she glanced at the hand enveloping the brown, wooden grip. Her hand, she thought, was a rough-knuckled fist ready to suffocate a sparrow. "My hands were made for something other than peeling shrimp," she said as she ran the tip of the blade down the incision, removing the black intestine.

"Roux?" her mother offered, pointing her own paring knife toward the hearth. "Make roux. I peel shrimp."

"Fine. Yes." Maggie drew up one side of her outer skirt, tucked it into her belt, and hoped she wouldn't be engulfed in flames when one of the ridiculous layers caught an ember.

Using heavy tongs, she removed the lid of the cast iron pot dangling from a hook and set it aside. Then, she poked at the burning logs until the fire came to life and licked the bottom of the pot. From a tub, she scooped out a generous portion of lard. It sizzled and spat as it hit the hot, black crock.

"Oh, thank you, Sabine," Maggie heard her mother say. "We be needing those soon."

Maggie turned her back to the fire and faced the maid. "And what do you think I should do with those?" Maggie asked pointing to the large onions in Sabine's dirty hands, then glanced at the debris trail that marked Sabine's footfalls from the door to the worktable.

"For the gumbo. As you asked," Sabine told her.

"They are covered in dirt. Do you like dirt in your gumbo? I don't, but maybe you half-breeds do. And you best look at me when I speak to you."

Sabine crossed to the pump and held one onion under the faucet. Just as she reached her hand toward the lever, Maggie exploded.

"Do not wash those in here, you twit! Take them outside, peel them, and then wipe off any dirt you see." After Sabine snatched the other onions off the table and turned to go, Maggie added, "After that, sweep your filth off my floor."

"Why must you be so cruel?" Josephine asked her daughter.

"If I am being forced to pay her, which I am, I can treat her however I choose. Perhaps I'd be kinder if she weren't dumb as that chicken right there." Using a wooden spoon, Maggie pointed through the window at a chicken pecking the dry dirt. "She should count her blessings that I provide her a broom." A brilliant fantasy appeared in Maggie's mind: Sabine on all fours licking the floor clean. "Yes, she should count her blessings," Maggie said with a hint of a grin.

She turned back to the pot and sprinkled flour over the melting lard with one hand while stirring with the other, now tethered to the pot until the roux was done. The heat from the fire crept beneath her skirts and climbed toward her stomach, chest, and face. She wiped her face with her sleeve, leaving a wet smear on her blouse, and continued to stir without stopping. She scraped the bottom of the pot, making sure not a speck of flour burned, forcing her to start the process anew.

Again, Maggie stared at her right hand. It gripped the long wooden spoon. With each circle, no matter how gently she attempted the motion, the pot swung against its handle, teased her, teetered back and forth, and threatened to, with any given scrape or swipe, flip and crash onto the fire below. No, her hands were not made for women's work. *Josephine's were. Sabine's could do nothing else*, Maggie thought, *but not my hands*. The hands of Marguerite Adele Alpuente Lawry were meant for something else.

If ever a woman was misnamed, it was Maggie. Such a sweet, graceful name, proved her daddy's hope that his baby girl would be a proper lady one day. A proper fool, Xavier Alpuente never examined Maggie's hands, the hands that so profoundly announced that he and Josephine had spawned no lady.

How disappointed he was to realize his Marguerite was more vinegar than sugar and that *sweet* would never describe his baby girl. Xavier wore his disappointment as an ill-placed coat, suffocating him in the punishing heat and humidity. Even more disappointment piled on when she refused the suitors her father lined up for her and chose instead to take up with the Lawry gang, an assemblage of thieves, swindlers, heavies, and sharpshooters who preyed on the wetlands, equally distributing their crimes among businessmen, farmers, and fishermen alike.

"No daughter of mine will live with those men," Xavier had told his only child. "Have you no respect for me, your mother, yourself?"

"I've got enough respect for myself to live as I want," Maggie told him. "Ray Don makes me feel as no other man ever—" Her wild-eyed justification disrupted with a sharp slap to her cheek. "I hope you don't expect me to cower in pain," she told him, glaring at him. In his eyes she saw weakness and regret. "You'll never do that again, will you, Daddy?" She turned and descended the front porch steps as a victor, hiked up her skirts, and hopped into the driver's seat of a wagon. For extra measure, she leaned to Ray Don, head reprobate, kissed him on the cheek, then waved goodbye to her father.

One year later, Maggie walked unmasked and alone into the Morganville Cooperative two counties over and then out again only three minutes later with a bag of crisp bills, all belonging to do-good farmers, plantation owners, and businessmen. The next day, she and Ray Don married beneath a canopy of river birch, oaks, and sycamore.

Did Xavier Alpuente blame himself for the path Maggie's life took? Did he regret taking six-year-old Marguerite into the damp woods and lining up her first deer down the barrel of the rifle?

He had wrapped his arms around the child that morning and helped her hold the heavy rifle.

"I can do it myself, Daddy." She shrugged off his arms and wriggled away from him.

"It's going to kick—"

"I know," she said, giving her father a snapped glance that by her tender age he knew meant she would not be deterred. She held the rifle straight, eased her breath, felt the strength in her forearm, bicep, and shoulder. Then, she pulled the trigger. She landed on her rear end with the mighty kick as the bullet left the chamber, but her kill shot landed in the crease above the deer's thigh and dropped him in an instant. Maggie responded with a look of satisfaction, as if the deer had done exactly as she'd willed it.

Rumor had it that Maggie's daddy dropped dead at the news of his firstborn grandbaby – the first legitimate child of Ray Don Lawry, general ne'er-do-well and Protestant, if any religion at all found space in his heart. For the devout Catholics of Huet Pointe such as Xavier and Josephine Alpuente, children were the blessings, purpose, and mortar of a marriage. The birth of the child surely meant the death of any hope to annul the marriage.

"Abomination," Xavier had proclaimed just before he clutched his chest and fell, face-first, to the floor. The wind carried the outburst from the front steps of the sainted church to every yearning ear throughout town.

The roux, through constant stirring, turned a fine chocolate brown without burning – a required skill of any Southern woman, one that Maggie begrudgingly possessed. From another dangling pot, she pushed aside chicken bones and tender meat with a ladle, then poured a spoonful of stock into the cast iron pot and continued to stir until the thick roux dissolved, creating a rich, brown broth. From the table, she grabbed a bowl of onion, celery, and peppers – a Holy Trinity chopped to perfection by Josephine's lovely hands. Maggie dropped them in the stew and gave the pot another stir, then turned back to the table, her mother, and the shrimp.

It was my plan, she thought, *Mine*. She picked up a shrimp and twisted the legs until the shell loosened.

"All we gotta do," she told Ray Don the previous evening, "is wait in the reeds until Smoky Mary approaches. When she passes, we run alongside the track. The women's car is always third in line. We'll hop on, wave a couple pistols at 'em and they'll empty their purses and corsets of whatever they're holdin'. They don't have a clue how to defend themselves. Trust me. It'll be the easiest prize yet." Maggie paced in front of Ray Don, too excited to sit.

"I've never robbed a train before. You're sure it won't be ridin' too fast?" Ray Don had asked.

"Nah, I spied it a few weeks ago, when I got word of the new engine. And Smoky Mary, according to everybody in town, runs a lot better than the old one. So, we don't have to worry 'bout it breakin' down. This engine just keeps on runnin' so there's no chance of the men being able to help the women. We jump on, take what we want from the heifers, and jump off. We'll be back in the reeds on our way here 'fore the men even know anything's up."

"We? No. *You* ain't goin' nowhere," Ray Don told her and stood from his chair, so she had to look up at him to respond.

"Excuse me?"

"You, Miz Lawry, ain't robbin' no train. You leave that up to me and the boys."

"You're not goin' if I'm not!" She stepped toward him, so close she could smell the whiskey on his breath. "It's my plan. My prize!"

"It was your plan and a damn fine one. So, thanks, pet." Ray Don patted her on the behind as he passed.

Maggie crossed to the doorway, using her body as a barricade. "I'm not your damn pet. I'm your wife. And I'm telling you I'm going!"

"You are my wife, and no wife of mine is jumpin' trains. You're gonna accept what your job is now or leave. Your job is here and –" Ray Don grabbed his crotch, but before a grin could fully crack his face, Maggie landed a punch to Ray Don's stomach, bending the man with the blow. She knew where he thought her second duty was but couldn't stand the thought of that being her place in life.

He straightened, grabbed her chin in one hand, and then tossed her aside.

Maggie braced herself against the wall. "You're an ass, Ray Don."

"I know." He stood close to her for a moment, staring at her face.

Maybe he waited to see if he'd finally made her cry, but one thing his bride never did was cry. Even when giving birth to babies one through four, she didn't cry. Screamed. Cursed. Threw things. Shot things.

"Maggie?" Ray Don's voice had come from the other side of the closed bedroom door, as if he were stooped in front of the handle with his lips on the keyhole. With the previous births, Ray Don dismissed Maggie's labor as something all women were born to bear, but her screaming alarmed Ray Don—louder with baby number four than babies one through three, which was loud enough to rattle the walls.

"Ray Don Lawry, if you open that door, I'll shoot you dead where you stand." Maggie reached for her Colt revolver. "I'm ready to become Widow Lawry whenever you are."

The midwife dropped to the floor, cowering behind the foot of the bed. "Miz Lawry, put that thing down!"

"Maggie?" Ray Don softly rapped on the closed door. "What's happening? Do I have another boy yet?"

Maggie fired off one shot. Splinters flew from the top of the door jam. "That's your final warning. Get!" Then, looking around the sparse room, "Oh, for Christ's sake, get off the floor. I'm not going to shoot you." Maggie took in a long breath, readying herself for the next contraction. "So long as you do your damn job right."

Maggie had missed on purpose. Everyone in Huet Pointe knew her to be the best shot in the bayou, even better than Ray Don. Minutes later she frowned when the midwife placed the baby in her arms. Ralph, she decided to call him. Blasted boy number four.

"I'll take my brandy on the porch," Ray Don told her, determining the debate done, and walked out of the room.

The argument played over and over in Maggie's mind as she stood over the shrimp. *Maybe*, she thought as she ran her paring knife along the wet, spongy back, *Maybe, I could leave a few of these intestines in his shrimp*. She wondered if the feces of a dozen or so shrimp might be enough to kill him. Slowly. Ray Don deserved a long, vile sickness; one day of misery for every time he thought about shoving her. Two days for every time he did.

"It wasn't supposed to be like this," she whispered.

"Like what, mon petit?" Josephine peeked into Maggie's peeled bowl. "Good. Good. They good. You do good." She patted her daughter's hand before crossing to the hearth to stir the gumbo.

"Oh," Maggie yelped, and bore down on the table for support. The second flutter of the morning wasn't a flutter at all. A full kick deep in her womb landed so well that pain shot from her rib down to her toes.

"Cherie?" her mother asked and rushed to her side.

"Fine, fine," Maggie said, brushing her mother's affection aside. "I'm fine." She picked up the paring knife. "Just thought I nicked myself."

A gaping wound from the knife would be a more welcomed malady than what loomed in her belly. With each pregnancy, the kicking—constant shots that bruised her insides—informed her of the condition. Maggie wasn't like other women. She wasn't forced into confinement one week of every month. Her monthly visitor was fickle. It was nothing for her to go two, three months without the reminder that she was, in fact, born a woman. So, as with all the others, that kick told her exactly how many months were left.

Maggie didn't think of every child as a blessing from the Virgin Mary, a jewel in her tarnished crown. She believed them to be yet another strap, one more reason for Ray Don to forbid her from doing what she loved best.

"You stay here," Ray Don had told her eight weeks after Ray Jr. was born. "My boy needs his mama close."

Maggie grew agitated, in need of anything other than rest, and she never liked playing house, even as a girl. This first tether aggravated her as if her boot caught a thicket.

With every child, her days of seeing the surprise in her target's eyes, resulting from the knowledge of being robbed by a woman, slipped further from her reach. Ruining the assumption that women were weak was her favorite part of life with the Lawry Gang.

After Philip, boy number two, Ray Don let out a chortle when Maggie handed the infant over to her mother and picked up her gunbelt. Philip wailed as she took one step away, his little face red and twisted with rage.

"Not so fast, Missus Lawry. My boys need you. Us men will take care of this one," Ray Don told her, then snatched her gunbelt from her and tossed it over his shoulder. No longer allowed the thrill of the hunt, the sweet satisfaction of knowing every second of a heist went according to her plan was robbed from her. Her very biology made her weak in his eyes.

As an exceptionally cruel joke, Ray Don had named baby boy number three Colt. "Now you've got a Colt of your own, something more appropriate for you to play with." Standing at Maggie's bedside, he glanced at his sweaty and exhausted wife, legs spent from hours of pushing. Ray Don checked the chamber of the Colt revolver in his hand, Maggie's revolver—the one he'd taken from her!— and holstered it. "We'll be gone a few days. Five tops." With that, Ray Don had kissed the newborn on the head and walked out of Maggie's bedroom.

Five? Five! This baby, kicking and stretching and ripening in her belly, wove a fifth rope to tie her to the house, to the kitchen. Four was enough to quarter her—one for each limb to yank to her the four corners. Four boys. A fifth surely meant the gallows with no hope of a last-minute pardon. Her life, as she used to know it, was done. Nightly, she begged God, any god, to return her to her former life, to allow her one more sin, one more run to satisfy the itch, but every morning she woke to mouths to feed and a house to run and a mother to tolerate.

Please let this one be a girl, she prayed. She couldn't handle another boy for Ray Don to display as his prize, to mold in his image. She needed a girl, one to take the women's work from her. A girl could free her, eventually. *Maybe she'll even look like me,* she thought. *Then the kitchen can have its proper Marguerite and Maggie will have, what? Even with a girl to do the women's work, would Ray Don take the old me back?*

She counted forward through the months. "December," she said, then ducked her head to avoid her mother's glance.

"Que?" her mother asked in her native tongue, a mistake commonly made from a lack of mindfulness.

"Nothing." Maggie picked another shrimp from the bowl and tore the head from the body. "Nothing."

And then she did the math that counted.

She counted back to nearly five months prior to Ray Don pushing her the night of their most recent argument. Five months before wind blew hot air into the kitchen. Before the kicking started. She counted back to the one moment she became, if only for a handful of breathless minutes, the woman she used to be. In that moment, behind the sainted church and next to the chilled water of the creek, a man had reminded her that the real Maggie still breathed. Her life could still be hers. Life on her own terms with moments to make her tremble as he rolled his R's in whispers against her neck. And even though that pious man would be hers for little longer than a moment, the child, part her lover, part her, would be hers forever—a piece of her rebellion to groom and shape to her liking.

Yes, she thought, yanking the legs free from another shrimp, *Let this be a girl.* She felt a smile on her face as she thought of what the little girl could be. Smart and bold like her. Pretty like Josephine. Steadfast as Xavier. *And her hands,* Maggie hoped, *may her hands be neither mine nor Ray Don's. May they not be Mama's or Papa's. Make them his hands. His smooth, bronze hands. And make*

Ray Don look at those hands and wonder if he should kill me or not. For the first time in over a decade, Maggie felt her prayer was authentic and heard. *And may her hands never do a day of women's work.* Maggie decided then and there to accept women's work if the baby was a girl.

As she ran the paring knife down the back of a shrimp, digging out the black bowel, she smiled. Her need to plot her revenge on Ray Don dissolved. That seed had already been planted and now ripened in her belly. The mere sight of her baby girl with bronze skin and a strong jawline may be enough to end Ray Don.

With the bowl of peeled shrimp pressed against her belly, Maggie crossed to the hearth. As she tipped the bowl and watched the fleshy, grey shrimp tumble over the lip and into the pot, she imagined a little girl splashing in Huet's Creek. She thought of the little girl watching her mother take aim at the old tree behind the house, spoiled from years of target practice. In her fantasy, the little girl squealed as Maggie hit the bulls' eye, then begged to try a shot herself. Maggie grinned as she stirred the gumbo and watched the shrimp turn from grey to pink.

"What is it, pet? You happy?" Josephine asked.

"I could be, Mama. Soon. I could be very happy." Then Maggie did the math again. Once more, and she was sure.

❄

Sabine 2

SABINE FREDIEU SMELLED of gardenia and incense, with a hint of chicken blood. It was the chicken blood she tried to hide as she twisted gardenia petals between her fingers and stuffed the torn bits into her bodice. She had plenty on which the ladies of Huet Point could and certainly would judge her. She didn't need the taunts of her adolescence - *Voodoo Witch! Ouanga!*

She wished she could put away the schoolyard taunts for good, having finished the eighth grade and her school days two years prior. She stuffed two more gardenia buds into the pocket of her apron and lifted her skirts just enough to ascend the steps of Hodges General Store.

The nuns of Our Lady of Sorrow Home for Wayward Children had certainly not taught Sabine the ways of the Nago, telling her to pray to the Virgin and Saints rather than the Iwa. They'd taken the child in, after all, barely old enough to speak when a young nun found her sitting just outside the convent door, sucking a strand of the yarn hair of a rag doll. Her mother, whomever she was, must have known the nuns would not allow the Vodou rituals to live within their walls. But the nuns couldn't control playground whispers—*Voodoo Hag! Witch!* And they couldn't control how Sabine's spiritual education evolved once free of the orphanage walls.

"You lost?" Mamba Loo had asked her two years before at this very spot, shortly after Sabine had arrived in Huet Pointe. "Them stairs ain't gonna bite," the old woman teased. An air of importance floated about the woman, a stark contrast to her dingy apron and skirt and tattered blouse.

Sabine had been standing at the foot of the Hodges' steps for ten minutes before the round, tall woman, the shape of a mighty oak, but soft, broke her concentration. Sabine glanced up from the chicken scratch list crumpled in her hand. Although fourteen at the time, full grown by most accounts, she wished to rest her head on the strange woman's black breast or belly. It looked a much better place to land than where she'd found herself the previous evening.

"No, Ma'am. I'm not lost," she told Mamba.

"Then what you doin'? You been staring at that paper then looking up at them doors for going on ten minutes now."

"You've been watching me?"

"Child, Huet Pointe is my town. I see some young thang I never seen before, I stop to make my ob-sa-vations. What else you expect? I got to know you ain't here to cause no trouble, but it looks like you's incapable of trouble."

"I need to get Miz Lawry's list done and—"

"Oh, you's *Sabine*. I heard Miz Lawry got her a new girl with a right pretty name. Help with all them brats running' round that place."

"Yes, Ma'am. I'm Sabine Fredieu." Sabine reached out a delicate hand to greet Mamba, just as the nuns had taught her.

"Well, you's right trained aren't ya? You might find not too many folks in this town share your manners. Especially at the Lawry's place. But I'm guessing you already figured that out." Mamba Loo reached one hand toward Sabine's face and lightly brushed the purple and green bruise below her left eye. "I'm Mamba Loo. And it appears you gonna be needing me."

Sabine glanced at the ground, her eyes moist.

"Now, don't you go tearin' up on me." Mamba stepped back and looked the young woman up and down. "You mixed?"

"Yes, Ma'am."

"Dat's what I heard. You got a hard road, but don't you fret none. Mamba will teach you good." Mamba's large teeth gleamed in the morning sun. Her smile formed a white bridge that nearly connected her large, squishy earlobes. "Get on now. We ain't got all day." Mamba Loo scooted Sabine toward the stairs and flitted her mammoth hands for Sabine to *get on up there.*

Sabine glanced at her list one last time, folded it, and walked up the three stairs. When she turned the handle and pulled the door open, she startled at the bell. Without looking up, she walked straight to the counter.

Reading from the list, she said, "Good morning, Sir. I will need two pounds of white flour, three pounds of white rice, two pounds of sugar, and one bag of dried beans." Sabine rattled off the items in one breath, no harsh tones, no mumbling. She had been *right trained.*

"Who exactly are you barking orders at, girl?" the shopkeeper, Mr. Hodges, asked.

Sabine glanced up. "I'm so sorry. I thought you were the man to help me. See, Miz Lawry gave me her list, and I need to get everything on it," Sabine said while digging in her pocket for her the purse Miz Lawry had entrusted to her. "See, she gave me money. Counted it out herself, and—"

"Stop chirping. My God! Just put the list on the counter and stand over there." Mr. Hodges raised one arm containing the widest bicep Sabine had ever seen and pointed to a corner several feet from the counter. "I best not see you touching anything. Everything in here is accounted for. And nothin' is for you."

As she scurried to her assigned corner, three white children thumbed their noses at her before returning to rummaging through a barrel of taffy candy wrapped in pink waxed papers. Sabine wished she could reach her hand in the barrel for one piece.

Just one piece like the piece she had two Christmases ago—a gift from a generous benefactor to the children's home.

After several minutes in the corner trying to be as quiet and still as humanly possible, hands folded neatly at her waist, Mr. Hodges reappeared with a large muslin sack. "Everything's here but I have one pound of sugar for Miz Lawry today."

"No, no, no," Sabine said, panic rising in her throat. "Miz Lawry said two pounds and I don't know what to tell her if I show up with only one."

"You tell her that's all I had, you stupid cow!"

Shaking, Sabine emptied the contents of the purse on the counter.

Mr. Hodges glanced at the coins and pushed one silver piece back toward the girl. "Take that back to Miz Lawry." He eyed Sabine as if she planned to keep the coin for herself.

Sabine lifted the heavy sack off the counter, nodded farewell, and braced for the bell to ring as she twisted the doorknob. When she glanced up, Mamba sat across the street, fanning herself in the shade and dangling her feet off the edge of a cafe porch. Her legs swung back and forth as if belonging to a girl of Sabine's age rather than the self-appointed ruler of the second and third classes.

"Got what ya needed?" Mamba called to Sabine. Without waiting for Sabine to respond, Mamba Loo hopped off the porch. "Come on." Mamba Loo turned and dashed through an alleyway.

Sabine, her arms pressing the sack of goods against her chest, caught up to Mamba, paused at a trailhead leading into the thick woods.

"Where are we going?" Sabine asked. Her question wasn't in protest. Sabine had no clue why she followed the near stranger, but she knew she needed to. She also thought it sensible to know where the old woman intended to take her.

"This here's a shortcut. Back to the Lawry's. I heard 'bout Miz Lawry's temper. So you got to get to gettin' after all that foolishness and staring on them steps. But I thought now's be a good time for yo' first lesson. Ain't no better place for learning than with the trees."

"Learning about what?"

"First, Mamba's gonna teach you how to survive in her town. From the looks at that shiner you got yo-self, you need some lessons."

Mamba talked the entire hour-long hike to the Lawry's, only pausing for an occasional breath. She spilled Huet Pointe gossip, which ladies in pink and green and pale blue to avoid, which ones were actually kind and good and decent and treated their maids, butlers, and nannies like actual human beings, and which men should cause Sabine's feet to sprint as she'd never ran before. Sabine's employer, Ray Don Lawry, held the top spot on Mamba's list.

Then, under the canopy of oaks, Mamba introduced Sabine to the Vodou Iwa and Nago traditions. "They's in your blood, Sabine. You can't deny 'em. You got to let 'em be. Let 'em in."

"But, Mother Superior told me I'd be condemned for all eternity..."

"*For all eternity* for something *in* you? That ain't right. You's created by God Almighty, and He," Mamba paused to point and smile at the heavens, "don't make mistakes."

Sabine halted and stared at the strange, dark woman. Mamba may have been spewing nonsense, but it was the sweetest nonsense Sabine had ever heard. And they were the first kind words to come her way since she hopped from the wagon that brought her to Huet Pointe. After a few contemplative moments, Sabine began to walk again, this time a little bit taller.

Hidden by pine, oak, and cypress, Mamba removed Sabine's tignon then wrapped it around her head so that it stayed in place all day—not a tempting, curly strand astray or a single follicle strained. After the dizzying hour, Sabine bade Mamba farewell and watched her scurry back into the tree line.

Two years after that first lesson and staring at those same three steps, Sabine touched the fresh bruise on her cheek and prayed Mamba would not notice it later that evening. She patted the pocket of her apron causing her purse to jingle-jangle against her hip as she ascended the three steps. A tinny ding-ding sounded as she crossed the threshold. In response, Sabine sucked in her lips, chewing a bit before exhaling.

Miz McLeary, a plantation owner's wife, impressive in sage hat, gloves, and dress, and near the top of Mamba's avoid-at-all-cost list, stood near the front counter. She and Mr. Hodges, clothed in his usual stiff white shirt, white apron, and grey britches, exchanged a frown. Sabine felt it in her bones. Every frown seemed to echo the accusations of "half breed" and "mulatto."

I am not a mule. I am not a mule. Sabine repeated the chant in her head as she fingered the purse in her apron pocket. *Can a mule dance? Can a mule sing? No, but I can. I am not a mule.*

Her purse held six dollars and fifty cents. Two dollars in coins was hers, equal to a full week pay as a domestic for the Lawrys. The other belonged to Miz Lawry.

"That's four dollars and fifty cents," Miz Lawry had told her that morning as she handed the purse to Sabine. "You best get there and back with my money right quick. No dawdling or picking flowers or casting spells on toads or whatever else you do in those woods when I'm not watching. Got it?"

"Yes, Ma'am," Sabine said, only glancing up at Marguerite Lawry's face for a second before staring at the floor again.

"And don't you come back here without every item. I'll have none of yours and Mr. Hodges nonsense today. My money is as good as everybody else's in this piss-ant town."

Once a week for two years, Marguerite Lawry had reminded Sabine, the *most useless twit* she'd ever known, of her egregious failure with the sugar.

Before crossing to the counter, Sabine reviewed the list once more, marveling at Miz Lawry's chicken scratch. In fact, she bet any one of the chickens cooped next to her shack had better penmanship. How a woman as mean as Marguerite Alpuente Lawry became the madam of a household, she couldn't figure. No matter how often Sabine glanced at her missus across the kitchen worktable or across the back lawn as she took her afternoon nap sprawled in a rocker on the porch, she couldn't imagine any man, even one as awful as Ray Don, choosing her. The nuns of Sabine's childhood would have tanned her hide for slouching in such a manner, sprawled with her legs open.

Sabine had chosen a white blouse, red striped skirt, white apron, and red headscarf for the day. The cotton of the tignon was dyed a deep, blood red and made of such a long stretch that she had to twist the fabric as she wrapped it around her head, carefully covering every strand so not to aggravate Miz Lawry, the other white women in town, the shopkeeper, or the sheriff and or his deputy. She shuddered to think how Mr. Lawry preferred her long, curly black hair pooled over her shoulders and down her bare, lean back to slender waist.

Sabine preferred to not think of Ray Don Lawry at all. Or his wife and her vicious moods.

The one charity Miz Lawry afforded Sabine was clothing. She refused to provide hats and gloves for her creole servant but did replace essential garments when skirts became tattered or elbows of sleeves threadbare. With each gift of a new blouse or skirt, the bitter matron chastised herself for being too generous. Miz Lawry bemoaned her kind spirit, loudly and often, and how if Sabine had any other missus, she would know real suffering. Sabine accepted each offering with a grateful smile and quiet thank you knowing all the while, the new blouse or skirt or tignon scarf had nothing to do with generosity and everything to do with the ego of a woman who felt the disapproving glances of the Huet Pointe elite in her bones, just as Sabine did.

With her head bowed, Sabine crossed to the counter, the list clenched in her hand. When she looked up, Miz McLeary gawked at her.

"As if she knows what those letters mean," Anna Beth McLeary said to Mr. Hodges.

"Oh, she's real uppity," Hodges sneered. "Supposedly, if you can believe a word out of her mouth, some nuns taught her to read at the orphan's home."

"Now, why in heaven's name did they do that?" Anna Beth asked.

Mr. Hodges chuckled, full and hearty so that his stomach bobbed up and down beneath his starched shirt and apron.

"And," Anna Beth said loudly enough to be sure Sabine heard her, "If I had such a desperate life that I took up with the likes of the Lawrys, I'd be a bit more modest. If you'll gather up my order, please. It's getting a little crowded in here for my taste." Miz McLeary eyed Sabine again, then turned her back with such flair her skirts swung back and forth like a bell.

As a child, Sabine conditioned her mind not to dismiss the insults of the ladies in sage or pink or periwinkle. She considered it part of her training. She knew that one day she would leave the nuns with their black and white habits and well-defined rules. But where do two halves of separate wholes belong? Her colorful half surely excluded her from her paler half, so on her fourteenth birthday Sabine chose to live in between, accepting the position of scullery maid to the Lawrys.

On the Lawry homestead, the family lived in the big house decorated with ostentatious fineries indicative of new money— Ray Don's ill-gotten gains. Ray Don's gang of miscreants slept in the bunkhouse. Even their quarters were finished with wrap around porches and oil lamps and proper outhouses with doors and latches. The black people, a mix of slaves and free mixed-race hands, lived in a shanty village of sorts along the backside of the vast property. Sabine's shack, private except for a few wandering chickens, lay just beyond the bunkhouse at the edge of the shanties.

Behind the shanty village thick woods shaded the banks of Huet's Creek. A twenty-minute stroll down the creek bank led to a sprawling plantation and another shanty village. Every colored man and woman, slave or free, knew of it and in which shack to find Mamba Loo with her sacred rattle and bells.

In the shop, Sabine checked her purse, counting the coins for the fourth time that morning. Two quarters were reserved for Mamba Loo. Those could not be spent. She prayed she'd saved enough.

"What's on your list this morning, girl?" Mr. Hodges asked. "Get what you need and get out."

"Yes, sir," Sabine said, polite even when Huet Pointe thrust its oft unkindness upon her. "Flour, coffee, and Miz Lawry's shirting order, please."

"How much?"

Sabine felt a panic build in her throat. "I'm not sure. Missus didn't tell me what the order was."

"The flour and coffee. How much flour and coffee?"

"Oh. Five pounds of flour, one pound of coffee."

"Wait here." The man waived one chubby finger at the corner, the colored people's corner as Sabine now thought of it. With the gesture, he might as well have told Sabine, "I know your kind, and your kind steals." Week after week, month after month, his silent insult had never changed.

Within a few minutes, he returned to the counter with two muslin sacks, one of coffee and one of flour, and a package wrapped in brown paper, tied neatly with a strand of twine. "Try not to wrinkle this on your way back home," he told her. "I don't want to hear about it from Miz Lawry." The one thing Sabine had in common with the white people of Huet Pointe was fear of Miz Lawry. "Four dollars, thirty-five."

Sabine counted out the coins in her purse and laid exact change on the counter one dollar and silver piece at a time. The shopkeeper glanced at the pile; Sabine assumed this was to check her mathematics.

"I'm going to need a few more things this morning." Sabine made eye contact with the man, but only for a second before glancing into her purse again. "Two cups of white rice, two cups of sugar, and one white candle please. The whitest you have."

"You got money for all that? I ain't givin' you no tab."

"Yes, sir. I have money."

"Stay here." Again, the man tapped the counter. After a minute, he returned with two small muslin sacks and a white candle.

"This candle has a dent in it. Do you have a different one? A good one?" Sabine asked.

"This candle is perfectly good. No, I don't have a different one. Not for you." He glanced at the items, and then said, "Fifty-five cents. You got that much in that purse of yours? I seen you hidin' it in that pocket of yours like somebody's gonna take it from you. As if that's how that works."

Sabine counted out fifty-five cents, laid the coins on the counter, and collected all of the items into a river reed basket. She waited for a moment to see if the shopkeeper gathered up the coins and put them in the register. As always, he didn't. Sabine had never seen him touch a single item she'd ever touched. Rather, he stood frozen behind his counter, neither smiling nor frowning. Sabine felt his eyes on her all the way out the door.

Mamba Loo, during one of her many lessons, had taught Sabine the art of walking with a basket balanced atop her head, allowing Sabine to double or triple her loads to and from town. So, with her basket resting on her head, the weight cushioned by her tignon, Sabine walked toward trailhead, choosing to take Mamba's scenic shortcut to the Lawry homestead. As soon as she stepped on the solitary path, with the sounds of Huet Pointe proper muffled by the trees, tall grass, and sugarcane, she sang to herself, for herself, and for the simple joy of singing.

> *Mary, you are holy, you are God's mother*
> *We are sinners, oh pray for us.*
> *Before we are serving the lwa, we first call upon God.*
> *Mary, you are holy, you are God's mother.*
> *We are sinners, oh pray for us.*

Her song carried her home, removing for a moment the worry that plagued her mind and pressed against her heart. Having eyed Miz Lawry snoring on the front porch, legs spread wide, mouth gaping, Sabine heaved the basket through the kitchen door near the rear of the house. Then she tucked her items, the chipped candle, rice, and sugar, in her apron pocket and scurried out, not stopping until she reached her shack.

The blazing sun finally dipped below the horizon as Sabine scrubbed, rinsed, and dried the dinner dishes, pots and pans caked with bits of blackened fish and griddle cakes, mixing bowls and utensils, four plates for the Lawry brats, three for her employers and Miz Lawry's mother, and nine for the half-drunk thugs. Her muscles ached as she ascended the stairs and wrestled the brats into nightshirts and beds. When she scurried past the parlor door, Miz Lawry's voice pricked her spine.

"Are they asleep?"

Sabine knew Miz Lawry posed the question to her. Pretending not to hear would result in more than a delay. "Yes, Ma'am, asleep." The door, askew on its hinges from her employers' most recent brawl, creaked as Sabine opened it. Miz Lawry lay on the embroidered sofa, a damp towel draped across her forehead. Miz Alpuente sat upright on a stool next to the sofa fanning her daughter.

"And Mister Lawry?" Miz Lawry asked.

"I don't rightly know, Ma'am. I haven't seen him since dinner."

"*You don't rightly know?* Useless." Miz Larry waved her mother away, pushing the fan down into the older woman's lap.

"May I get you something, Ma'am? Something to help you sleep?"

"I don't need a damn thing—" Miz Lawry sat up and twisted toward Sabine. She held her hand to her bloated belly. "Just go. Go do whatever it is you people do after you've—"

"Mon petite," Miz Alpuente said, coaxing her daughter to recline on a cushion, "you must try to be calm. The baby needs you to rest."

Watching Josephine Alpuente care for her daughter with such tenderness confounded Sabine. How could a woman so lovely, so gentle, produce such a hateful child? Miz Alpuente glanced up at Sabine with kind eyes and tight lips. She waved Sabine away then focused again on her daughter.

Sabine paused, breathing for a second to squash the urge to sprint away then she turned and walked straight through the kitchen and out the door. In her shack, she gathered her supplies into a small cotton sack and tucked the sack in one of the large pockets of her apron. Next, she grabbed the white garments, secretly pressed and hung earlier that day. She pulled the door closed behind her as she stepped into the moonlight, then hurried toward the trees.

Behind several red maple trees and button willow bushes, currently being choked out by honeysuckle blooms, Sabine removed her red tignon. Then she dropped her striped skirt to her ankles and stepped out. Hastily, as to not be discovered, she pulled the solid white skirt over her undergarments, tucked her white blouse into the skirt, and began wrapping a bright white tignon around her head. Pure white for Dambalah.

"Sabine, you here?" a whispered yell came from the trees nearest the creek.

Sabine looked through the bushes to see Mamba Loo standing next to the potomitan, the tree she had chosen for the holy ritual. Around the live oak, Mamba Loo would call upon Dambalah, the Iwa of creation, life, rain, snakes, and water.

"I will devote my life to Dambalah," Sabine had told Mamba Loo the night she first asked for the ritual. "In return, I know my Dambalah will protect me. He will protect me from both of them."

In the earth before the impressive tree, Mamba Loo drew. Her finger carved a large, diamond pattern with long tentacles and intricate spindles and curves. She then stood and held her open palm to Sabine.

Sabine dropped two silver coins in her hand, at which Mamba Loo frowned. "Is this all you have to offer me?"

"Please, Mamba, please."

"Don't you understand what Dambalah will bring you tonight? Don't you value the protection, the peace he will bestow upon you?"

"I value it more than life. Please."

Mamba Loo stood for several moments, gazing upon the petite Sabine. She touched Sabine's chin and raised her face into the moonlight, gazing into her eyes. "I believe you to be pure in heart. I believe you need this more than I need your coin. Those cursed with such beauty often find themselves in need." Then Mamba kissed two fingertips and pressed them against the bruise on Sabine's cheek—a purple blossom shining under the moon.

"Thank you, Mamba, thank you." Sabine kissed the old woman's hands until Mamba Loo retreated, seemingly uncomfortable with such a show of affection and appreciation.

In need, indeed. Sabine's needs were far greater than she could ever reveal to Mamba Loo.

"Please forgive me," Sabine had said to Miz Lawry two nights prior. The mistress of the house towered over Sabine near the hearth of the kitchen, too near. She feared that at any moment Miz Lawry would shove her into the fire. "I'm so sorry." Sabine dropped to her knees, tugging at her mistress's skirts, begging forgiveness for a sin she'd never wanted, certainly never intended. "Please, please. I don't want him. Please forgive me."

"Of course you want him. That's what whores do." Miz Lawry's voice seemed to retreat into the fire, coming from somewhere below the embers.

"I promise. I do not want him."

"You will." Miz Lawry bent down and yanked Sabine's chin toward her with one graceless paw. "You will want him, and you will take him every time he comes to you. If not, you will burn." Miz Lawry glanced at the fire and then, by way of Sabine's chin, shoved her to the ground. Then she stepped over Sabine, grabbed the bottle of rum from the shelf, and strolled out of the kitchen.

Afraid to move or speak or cry, Sabine had laid in the dirt and smut of the kitchen floor for nearly ten minutes.

In those ten minutes she decided to act, but not alone. Her precious nuns tried to steer her from the Nago, prevent curiosity with a solid dose of Catholicism, but sometimes, as Mamba Loo taught her, blood is blood and must be honored. Sabine knew it was time to call upon the Iwa as the nuns called upon the Holy Saints.

And by that night, the night she spent shivering on Mrs. Lawry's floor, Sabine had confessed the same sin so often she doubted the priest or any Catholic God believed in her ability or desire to repent. So really, what choice did she have, but to call upon her fellow Nago and Manmba Loo? Joining herself to Dambalah may be her only chance at peace.

"Our Father, Who art in heaven," Mamba Loo stood before the mighty tree and recited the Lord's Prayer as other woman with dark faces and white garments came from all directions to form a circle around Sabine.

"Merci, Merci," they whispered with the ending of each prayer, first the Lord's Prayer, then a Hail Mary, and finally, the Apostles' Creed.

"Merci, Bon Dieu. Thank you, Good God." Mamba Loo raised her rattle and began twisting her wrist. "Bon Dieu, let me call upon your servant, Dambalah."

"Merci, Merci," the women chanted as the priestess shook her rattle and shuffled her bare feet in the dirt.

"Shhhhhhhhhh," Mamba Loo silenced the women. "I am listening to you, Damballah, ma cher. Let me hear your voice. I will be still and listen to hear the voice of Damballah. I am confused and uncertain. I need your guidance and wisdom on ma petite, Sabine. Fill me with your peace and serenity. Whisper in my ear, great Damballah. Shhhhhhhhhhhhhhhhhh. Merci!"

Sabine, with the women, chimed in, shuffling their feet and dancing beneath the tree. "Shhhhhhhhhhhhhhhhhhh I am listening to you Damballah, ma cher. Let me hear your voice. I will be still and listen to hear the voice of Damballah. I am confused and uncertain. I need your guidance and wisdom. Fill me with your peace and serenity. Whisper in my ear, great Damballah. Shhhhhhhhhhhhhh. Merci!"

Sabine closed her eyes and raised her arms to the heavens, chanting with the women as sweat began to form under her chin and breasts. Then, at her feet, a hissing sound began. When she opened her eyes, she found Mamba Loo slithering on the ground, rubbing her body over roots and through the sacred drawing.

"Damballah," the women cheered. "Damballah is here!" They grabbed Sabine, lifting her over their heads. "Damballah has come for you!"

They lowered Sabine to the ground and handed her the offerings, for Damballah was ready to feed. First, Sabine fed him a boiled egg, of which he swallowed whole as a snake. Next, came the rice pudding. The sweet pudding dripped down his chin, but with a flick of his tongue he brought the dollop back to his mouth.

With each mouthful the women cheered, dancing around Sabine and Damballah, offering more eggs and pudding. When Damballah appeared satisfied, a thin woman, frail with age, stepped from the circle. "Sabine, my child, Damballah is ready for you."

"Yes." Sabine spoke her one-word agreement as tears pooled in her eyes.

"Do you take Damballah to be your spouse?" the woman asked. "Will you love him, honor him, obey him, until death?"

"I do. I will." With Sabine's response, the women fell silent, turning their gaze to Damballah.

"Do you Damballah, protector of life and peace, loving father to the world, do you take Sabine to be your spouse? Will you love her, cherish her, protect her until death?"

Mambo Loo, still ridden by Damballah, flicked her tongue once more, screaming, "I will!"

"Merci! Merci!" The women fell upon Sabine, kissing her cheeks till they were wet.

When Sabine emerged from the throng, Mamba Loo reached out for her hand, spent from the ritual. "Did he come to you? Do you belong to him?"

"Yes." Sabine cried. But her tears were not of fear or of a desire to be more than a mule, more than the mulatto trash this world had cursed her to be, more than Ray Don Lawry's whore and Mrs. Lawry's whipping post. For with her ethereal spouse, her Iwa, Sabine knew the sins of Ray Don and the curse of his wife were of the flesh alone. Her soul, the half of her that mattered, belonged to God Almighty.

❈

Part Two: Fall

Rosarie

RUTH WHITE FLOATED IN THE BAYOU, or rather her torso did. Still clad in her favorite, emerald green corset with lavender embroidered buds—water hyacinths floating on a bloated Lilly pad—the torso listed as if tugged at from beneath the slick surface. The mangled brocade, shredded in places, sliced as if by razor in others, bore the evidence of her journey from the swamp. Around the twists and turns of the brackish river. Slipping past cypress trees and patches of dying sawgrass. At last brushing against a sea-worn buoy just as a sleepy crabber bent to check his first trap of the morning. The bayou, glistening with the first rays of the day, seemed to take pleasure in its most unpleasant "How do?" that morning.

Two miles north of the foul remnant and two weeks after the grisly discovery, Rosarie Hodges sat on a bench in the hallway of what passed for law and order in Huet Pointe. She thumbed her monogram stitched in silk thread on a fine linen handkerchief. The thread so delicate, Rosarie barely felt it through her thin gloves. She'd been waiting over an hour and would wait no longer. Leaving was out of the question.

Just as she stood to adjust a naughty bone in her pale peach bodice, she heard the floorboards moan, whining as each footfall tested its structural integrity. The door flung open, creating a vacuum of ego and sweat, although the October breezes blew that morning. Sheriff Benjamin Tuckey plowed through, winded from whatever had kept Rosarie waiting so long, his belly heaving with every labored step.

"You again?" he asked, plodding past her without the slightest attempt at eye contact.

"Sheriff Tuckey, if I could have one or two moments of your time. I need to discuss a most pressing matter with you."

"Let me guess, you still believe your husband's whore was murdered?"

Rosarie flinched. "I will ask that you not use such words around me or about my husband."

"I hope you don't think ol' Hodges tuckin' into Madam White's establishment every Thursday afternoon went unnoticed. That was the worst kept secret in this town. And this town is full of poorly kept secrets."

Rosarie crumpled the handkerchief in her fist, resisting the urge to pommel the portly lawman where many a whore had explored with painted nails and stained lips and, hopefully, Rosarie thought, full purses; such a grotesque deed should be amply rewarded. "You need to hear what I have to say. I have critical information pertinent to Miss White's death."

"So, you asked Tarasque if he enjoyed his meal and he told you he didn't devour her? Was she too salty for his fine palette?" After a bit of jangling, Tuckey twisted a key in a lock, popping the door to his private office open.

"That gator did not kill Miss White!" The sudden rise in Rosarie's voice made her queasy. On any other day, she could have calmed herself before her emotions ran amuck, but not on the second Thursday following Ruth White's untimely demise. Rosarie closed her blue-grey eyes for a moment, taking one, two cleansing breaths. When she opened her eyes again, Sheriff Tuckey stared at her.

"Okay, okay," Tuckey propped the door open with a rock, then sat behind an oak, roll top desk. "The last thing I need this morning is a hysterical woman."

Rosarie stood in the open doorway, waiting for Tuckey to mind his manners and invite her to sit. "The craftsmanship of your desk is superb. The town council outdid themselves finding such a piece for you. I'm sure you won't disappoint them by allowing a murderer to roam our streets. Not after such a splendid gift."

"Why don't you have a seat?" Tuckey relented, but refused to hide his contempt.

With barely space enough for the desk, two chairs, her impressive triangle of skirts and petticoats, and Tuckey's belly, which required the desk to sit an extra foot from the wall, Rosarie navigated the office. She lowered herself into a wooden armchair, thankful for the plush cushion. She hoped the pain in her abdomen was in fact due to the naughty boning, a wayward soldier, and not another poisoned spot deep within her useless womb.

"So what is this critical information you have for me?"

"Miss White was not killed by an alligator, as you and others have assumed."

"Judging from the teeth marks in what was left of her, she most certainly was."

"Sir, her body may have fallen victim to Tarasque, surely only a creature that large could have devoured her, but he didn't kill her. Something or someone else is responsible for her body being in the water."

Tuckey leaned back in his chair and patted his belly with oddly small hands. "And what makes you so sure of that? What theory have you concocted in that imaginative brain of yours?"

"Ruth White learned to swim before she could walk."

"So? Perhaps that gator saw a plump treat standing near the edge and drug her in. Wouldn't be the first swimmer he ate."

"That too is impossible." Rosarie pressed her handkerchief beneath her upturned nose, hoping the jasmine essence overpowered the man-stink hanging in the air.

Sheriff Tuckey released an audible afterthought of sausage and coffee. "And why is that?"

"Are you not aware of Ruth's upbringing? She was born a Pellerine, not a White. All the Pellerine children might as well have crawled from the swamp suckling sawgrass reeds."

For twelve years straight, just as the choking heat eased with fall, Miz Pellerine's broad hips released a baby. Another gator hunter to accompany Mr. Pellerine, balanced on a pirogue, gaze fixed on the water. Two more hands to bait the hooks. Fourteen sets of hands in all, calloused from the thick scales, scarred from wrenching lines.

"And Ruth was smack dab in the middle of all those children, five older, six younger. I don't think her parents noticed or cared when Ruth decided she wanted something other than the swamp and hunting alligators all day long. I'm sure Miss Pellerine got to the business of replacing Ruth with great efficiency. I don't blame Ruth's mother, though. That life can't be easy. Children may have been the only joy she could find."

"What does any of this have to do with how Ruth died?"

"No Pellerine would fall victim to an alligator. They know them too well."

"You seem to know a lot about her and her family."

"I know everything about her."

"Really? You a Pellerine, too?"

"Of course not. But Ruth White was important to me. Very important."

"Well, now I am intrigued."

"I guess you could say Miss White and I had an arrangement. One of great benefit to my marriage."

"Really?"

"I believe there are certain things a wife should provide her husband. When I became unable to provide all that a wife should, I sought the assistance of Miss White."

"You mean you…"

"Yes, Sheriff Tuckey, I hired her. Seems our arrangement was the best kept secret in town." Rosarie pursed her cupid's bow together and inhaled a drag of jasmine from her handkerchief. "In doing so, I got to know her very well." Rosarie grimaced, but not from regret. She grimaced at the thought of the woman, or rather a portion of the woman, responsible for keeping one of Huet Pointe's most revered marriages intact, bobbing, headless, in the bayou.

"I must confess, Miss Hodges," Ruth White had told Rosarie so many years before her untimely death, "I've never seen such a thing. And here I's thinking I'd seen it all." Ruth waved the list just below Rosarie's nose. "Take a whiff, won't you? That's what astonishment smells like."

"I don't think you're in the position to mock me. My money is just as good as any of the men whose patronage you enjoy." Rosarie held her ground, refusing to reveal the speed at which her heart pounded against her breastbone.

"I've never claimed to *enjoy* any of my patrons." Ruth then scanned the list of Mr. Hodges needs, each concern penned in Rosarie's lovely, artful script. "So, am I supposed to chat him up each week? I've never been much for the flowery sentiment and long conversations. I prefer more *active* solutions."

"He's not the type of man to lay down with a woman for only carnal purposes. My Mr. Hodges will need some convincing before breaking his vows. You will have to convince him, befriend him."

"Oh, Miss Hodges, it's very sweet you believe that and fortunate for me that you do. So many of the wives of Huet Pointe believe in fidelity as you do. So, so many of you are wrong."

"I am unable to," Rosarie paused, searching for the least indelicate words to describe her predicament, then decided on, "marital relations have become a very painful endeavor for me. The least I can do is provide Mr. Hodges with a suitable, albeit untraditional, alternative."

"Don't worry, honey. I'll treat 'em right." Ruth White folded the list then tucked it between her ample breasts and corset lining.

Rosarie, fighting the burning humiliation of the conversation, marveled that anything other than the ample, spilling cleavage, even a folded piece of paper, could fit in Ruth White's corset. She also spent her entire walk home praying Mr. Hodges still thought her beautiful after he nuzzled against Ruth White's impressive bosom.

"I needed her to provide more than just a weekly ... tryst," Rosarie told Sheriff Tuckey. "I needed him to have someone to fulfill his needs, ones I could not. Between the two of us, Mr. Hodges became manageable."

Sheriff Tuckey expelled a choke.

"Should I fetch you a sip of water? More coffee, perhaps?" Rosarie asked.

"No, no. I'm fine."

"Lovely. So, I know for a fact Miss White was not killed by Tarasque, or any other swamp beast, for that matter."

"You having an arrangement—one I gotta say more wives should arrange just for public safety's sake—doesn't mean Miss White was murdered. Unless, of course, *you* intend to confess."

"No, Mr. Tuckey, I did not kill her, and I don't know who did. But I do know when she was killed. From there, you can conduct a proper investigation."

"Hold on, I ain't said there would be or wouldn't be an investigation. You tell me what you think you know, then I'll decide."

"Something, something awful happened to her just after three o'clock two Wednesdays past."

"That's a pretty precise estimate."

"Yes, it is. And an accurate one. You see, every Wednesday morning, I write a list of my husband's concerns. Anything that is frustrating him, aches and pains he may have, worries plaguing his mind. Perhaps the price of sugar has gone up or a shipment was late. Delayed shipments make for a flood of exacerbated customers. And, he has a bad shoulder you know. That plagued him for years. Nothing I offered gave any relief. I feared he'd keel over dead from the stress, but Miss White ... So, I write the list every Wednesday then roll the paper tightly and tuck it in my sleeve. At two every Wednesday afternoon, I set out on a stroll. At two forty-five, I sit on one of the benches near the church and read. That little patch always has something in bloom, no matter the season. At three, Miss White sits on the other bench. On my bench, on the end of the second plank, well, it has a hole in it. Every Wednesday at three I place the rolled-up list in that small hole. Then, I leave. Every Wednesday at three-fifteen, per our arrangement, Miss White switches to my bench, sits, and retrieves the list. For seven years we've done this. Never has the list been ignored or forgotten. Not once until two Wednesdays past." Rosarie pulled a rolled paper, two inches long and the width of a fountain pen, from her sleeve. "This is the note I left two Wednesdays ago. Two Thursdays ago, Mr. Hodges arrived at our home three hours early and in such a mood. Foul as a rotting gar saying that Miss White was nowhere to be found."

"Mr. Hodges knew of your arrangement?"

"Of course, he did. I would never go behind my husband's back. What a terrible thing to suggest."

"Yes, yes, of course."

"So, I got Mr. Hodges out back shooting targets, which helps alleviate his burdens, but aggravates his shoulder so that he can't shoot as often as he'd like. So yes, I made him as happy as I was able then went to look for Miss White myself. I was beside myself. That level of negligence was uncharacteristic of her and completely unacceptable. She'd always been trustworthy, dependable, despite her choice of profession. And because of that negligence I had to walk through that door into that parlor, that den of depravity for a second time! Looking for her among those gaudy brocade curtains and painted women made my skin prickle, but I needed to know why on earth Miss White, after seven years, dismissed our agreement. She knew how important Thursday afternoons were to Mr. Hodges. To me."

"So, did you find her?"

"Of course not. By that time a considerable amount of her was more than likely in Tarasque's belly."

"Except the bit floating south."

"Do you really think it wise to mock her demise—such a terrifying end?" Rosarie's glare slapped Tuckey, forcing him to straighten his slack posture. Satisfied with the adjustment, Rosarie continued, "When I could not find her in that godless house, I went to the church to check the bench. Something told me to check the bench. Sure enough, I found my note, unbothered, unmoved." Rosarie stood, the combination of naughty boning and whirring thoughts preventing her from sitting still another minute. (If only she'd room to pace!) "She was there on Wednesday at three. I saw her. Nodded to her and left the note. She saw me. She nodded back. So I ask you, what happened after I left that prevented her from retrieving the note? She would never ignore me. Never. Good or bad, right or wrong, I was her best paying customer. She said so herself. Why did she suddenly choose to ignore me? Break our deal? She wouldn't. She didn't. So you see, something must have happened to her just after I left her that day."

Tuckey's expression changed from perfunctory to a hint of suspicion. "And I've never seen a gator that far from shore before, unless of course we'd had a big rain. Which we haven't in a while."

"So, you understand why I am suspicious?"

"Yes. Something does seem off here."

"And the newspaper article did not mention her brooch. The reporter spoke of green brocade, but nothing of her brooch. Surely a brooch that lovely would be included in the description of the remains."

"Brooch?"

"She wore a sapphire and glass brooch on her lapel. Every day since the Wednesday before Christmas, 1845. The day I gave it to her. Mr. Hodges and I had had such a pleasant year, and I knew she was largely to thank. So, I ordered the brooch all the way from Boston for her."

"Very generous."

"Sheriff, you've no idea the changes Miss White made in our marriage. Before Miss White and Thursday afternoons, Mr. Hodges was so tense. Well, you know how men can be sometimes. They have needs. Needs that should only be met in the marital bed. So, when I found I could no longer fulfill those needs, which I must say distresses me to admit and I apologize to speak of such matters, but you are a man of the law so you should be kept abreast of everything, correct?"

"Correct," Tuckey said, appearing a bit worried. Perhaps Rosarie's anguish was contagious.

"I feared our union suffered so, maybe to the point of breaking. Miss White became the solution I prayed for." Rosarie returned to her seat, trouble weighing on her chest and taxing her corset bindings.

Sheriff Tuckey managed a sympathetic expression. "No. They didn't find a brooch. But so little of her was left."

Rosarie flinched again with the image.

"It could be on the bottom of the swamp or bayou or Huet's Creek. Lord only knows. Honestly, Ma'am, it could be jammed between Tarasque's teeth. That's a definite possibility."

"Find that brooch, and I bet you will find her killer."

"Well, short of prying that beast's mouth open…"

"Find it."

"How?" Tuckey's question was earnest. His first one of the day.

"Perhaps you should start with Miss White's girls. One of them must know something." Rosarie stood and tucked her handkerchief and the rolled list beneath the cuff of her fitted sleeve. "Meanwhile, I have to find and educate a new Thursday girl. I asked the one that's running the place now to take care of Mr. Hodges. She laughed in my face. Very rude that one. Not worthy of Mr. Hodges in the least." Rosarie crossed through the open office door, then waited for Tuckey to open the front door. "I trust you will be discreet with all I've told you today. And please, proceed with some sense of urgency. If not for the knowledge that a sinister being is roaming our streets, which is terrifying, investigate Miss White's death for me and the awful strain this has caused me."

Rosarie stepped through the door and glided down the street. Several doors down, she paused, bracing against a column as she reached for the door to Dann Hall Saloon and Café, as the new, freshly painted shingle announced. Inside, she breathed into her raised handkerchief, sizing up each tacky maven before her.

Anna Beth

WOMEN ONLY LEFT HUET POINTE in three forms: blushing bride, rotting corpse, or widowed burden to a married child. *Two decades past bride and I'm not ready for the crypt, so neither of those will do*, Anna Beth thought as she removed the handkerchief from her sleeve and, careful not spill its contents, tucked it beneath lace-trimmed petticoats in the bottom drawer of her mahogany chifferobe.

Never wanting to miss an opportunity, she thought it wise to keep a stash of the small, yellow beads nearby. The Angel's Trumpet she had cultivated from a seedling two decades before was in full bloom displaying the odd nature of autumn in Huet Pointe, but the blooms were as fickle as her womb. Overnight, they could fall to the ground; their precious gold spilt. Better to capture the pollen before it disappears. And so, on a stroll through the garden, Anna Beth had tapped and tapped and tapped a bloom until the yellow dust cascaded from the white bloom into her cupped handkerchief.

She stepped from her bedchamber onto her balcony and peered over the railing. Below, the lovely bushes, her first babies, her pets, were marvelous. The blooms reminded her of hand bells. They seemed to be waiting for their director to raise his hands, count off a rhythm. *All together now.* At any moment, a change of light, a breeze maybe, would prompt them to raise their heads to the heavens, a symphony of one hundred blooms.

"Oh!" Anna Beth startled as her maid and best confidante tapped her on the shoulder. "You nearly scared me to death, Tilly.

Please do walk a little louder so I won't jump out of my skin and over this railing! Or perhaps I should get you a bell. I could have impaled myself on my babies below, you know."

The thick stems of the Angel's Trumpet were stiff but hardly enough to pierce the skin. Tilly smiled at Anna Beth's outburst.

"Well, what is it?" Anna Beth asked, steadying her nerves.

Tilly motioned to the door, wagging an impatient finger. Anna Beth had been lost in a fantasy for too long.

"Oh, let me guess. I've been summoned to the parlor by my mother and the Leech?"

Tilly nodded.

"Just because she bore my husband does not mean she has the privilege to summon me. This is my house, not hers."

Tilly pressed her palms together, her way of saying, *please, please.*

"Fine, fine." Anna Beth stepped inside and crossed to the gilded mirror, nearly ten feet in height and five feet wide. Her eyes went first to the reflection of her skirts, sage green and massive with underpinnings and petticoats. As her gaze rose on her body, she smiled approvingly at her corset. "We must schedule that new girl at Hodges for another dress. Perhaps a darker green this time. Emerald green. Not sage like this one. This pale green is a bit passive for me. Don't you agree?"

Tilly nodded.

"It took twenty years, but this cesspool finally has a decent dressmaker." Anna Beth turned her attention to her own reflection again. "This dress really could be from Virginia; don't you think so?" Anna Beth paused for a nod from Tilly. "That girl did exquisite work with the boning. No one can tell I no longer have a waist." She stared at her maid, more precisely at Tilly's tiny waist. "You're so lucky to have never had children. My body never recovered from that last one, poor thing."

Tilly stood as near to Anna Beth as she could, what with all the layers of fabric between them, and glanced at their shared reflection. Her eyes seemed to glisten with sympathy. Anna Beth reached for Tilly's hand and squeezed it.

"Oh, I do wish you could make that twisted tongue of yours work." Then, Anna Beth's expression lost its kindness. "But, then again, maybe it's better this way." She peered at the mirror again, leaning closer to examine her face for one maybe two seconds. "Have Mamba Loo here in the morning. Tell her to bring the full arsenal. Something must be done about these pores." Then she turned on her heel and strutted through the doorway.

Left to her natural, God-given appearance, Anna Beth was a forgettable kind of pretty. Nothing objectionable. Her features were all pleasant and in the right form and place, but there was nothing remarkable, nothing striking to make the men, or more importantly the women, of Huet Pointe or her beloved, far off Richmond, Virginia, want her or want to be her.

Fortunately, Gill McLeary had just enough wealth to keep Anna Beth in all the latest fashions and nearly pickled by Mamba Loo's special salves and potions. The combination made up for a lack of God-given talents. Unfortunately, Gill McLeary made his wealth and home in Huet Pointe, which caused Anna Beth daily distress. The dirt roads, muddy with the constant rain, the Cajun slang, the hummingbird-sized mosquitos, the gross amount of file` spice mixing with piles of dead fish; her Virginia blood never acclimated. And the humidity! Tilly peeled the corset from Anna Beth's skin nightly; the flesh embossed with red boning lines and puffed from the steam and sweat.

Descending the stairs, she heard the pecking, back and forth from her mother to the Leech. Anna Beth attempted a deep breath, but the bindings of her ensemble prevented such a luxury. A too-loud sigh escaped her lips.

"Anna Beth, must you keep us waiting?" her mother's voice bellowed from the front parlor, a room decorated completely in mauve. Gil had insisted Anna Beth include his mother in choosing the décor for the grand house. After much discussion, Anna Beth offered a compromise: The Leech could have one room. Never did she dream of drapes, settees, rugs, even two, carved walnut armchairs doused in the flaccid pink. Pink ruined by brown. Pink ruined by indecision. *Mauve!* Anna Beth knew the old bag chose mauve just to spite her.

"Mother, Mother McLeary, what is all the pother? I could hear your bickering all the way upstairs."

"These," Mother McLeary, the Leech, motioned to the fabric swatches on the oval, high-lacquer coffee table. Next to the swatches lay a sketch of a ball gown with puffed sleeves, full skirt, and a plunging neckline.

"My offense is not with the fabrics," Anna Beth's mother declared. "It's the design that has me close to retching."

"Mother, you are, as always, right. In fact, Tilly," Anna Beth snapped her fingers toward Tilly who in return hurried to her side. "Please dismiss Chloe. Tell her she's free to return to whatever swamp she came from. I'd like the new girl at Hodges to take this over." Tilly retrieved a pencil and pad from her apron pocket as Anna Beth dictated instructions. "Tell her absolutely no puffed sleeves. So passé. Rather the sleeve should skim the arm just past the elbow. The neckline should be boxed, not too low, and a full corset like the one I'm in now. And I'd like to approve her sketch tomorrow. The porter will take you into town." With her orders complete, Anna Beth dismissed Tilly, not considering the fact that by the time her maid reached Hodges General Store, it may very well be closed for the day, forcing Tilly and the porter to track down the seamstress wherever she may be. Returning with the task incomplete was unacceptable.

"Oh, and all white, different shades, but white on white on white!" Anna Beth called after Tilly.

"But she'll look like a bride." The Leech often found fault with Anna Beth's choices when it came to her only granddaughter. This time was no different.

"That's the point. A proper preview. What do you think we're doing this for?"

"White should be reserved for *the* day." The Leech straightened her spine, attempting to stretch her frame to Anna Beth's height.

"And mauve should be reserved for the satin." Agreeing on fabric choices with the woman responsible for the hideous parlor was not an option for Anna Beth. In fact, the old hag's disapproval confirmed Anna Beth's choice of all white for the dress. She waited for Mother McLeary's fat nostrils to stop flaring then lowered herself onto the settee, spreading the sage green of her skirts over as many mauve forget-me-nots as possible. "Now that the dress is settled," Anna Beth said cutting her brown eyes toward her mother-in-law, "let's move on to the guest list."

Both widows nodded, although Mother McLeary appeared singed around the edges.

Anna Beth angled herself toward a seating chart placed on an easel. "Are these all the confirmations we've received?" This was a rhetorical question, of course. Anna Beth allowed no one in the household to look upon the responses except Tilly and herself. And, Tilly was as safe a bet that Anna Beth could make against the spread of insidious rumors. She turned her attention back to the Leech. "Not a single *yes* has come from New Orleans. I thought between your family connections there and Gil's business connections, at least a handful of families would attend. Or, are those supposed influences of yours complete balderdash? Something certainly is rancid here."

"Give them a bit more time to respond. Perhaps Bonnie's debut is not—"

"Not what? Important?" Anna Beth's pitch rose with the thought of anyone not understanding the gravity, the pressure of her only daughter, only child, making her debut. So much hung on one dress. This was the one evening to prove Bonnie's worth, and Anna Beth's one chance at salvation. If Bonnie could not marry well, Gil's planned and untimely demise would be for nothing. How many handkerchiefs, stained yellow, had she been through? "Of course, *you* would excuse their behavior. If they cannot be bothered to respond, you will go to New Orleans. Arrange a tea and demand a response. Tomorrow. You will go tomorrow."

"Anna Beth, that is not how things are done," the Leech said. "And you'd be wise to remove that tone from your voice when speaking to me."

"Gran Mere`, mother's just a bit tense," Bonnie said, appearing between the columns of the parlor entryway, "Mother, I'm sure we will receive responses in good time. No need to send Grand Mere` traipsing across the bayou."

Bonnie McLeary, clad head to toe in powder blue, a lovely shade for her creamy skin, blonde hair, and sky-blue eyes—the kind that cause men to take up arms—allowed a sweet smile to settle below her perfectly pert nose.

No, Anna Beth's only child was in no way a forgettable kind of pretty. She was a striking beauty, a portrait of grace and vitality in powder blue as she tucked herself between her grandmothers on the mauve sofa, kissing both on the cheeks as she did. Bonnie glanced at her own mother and smiled as if to say, "Be kind, mother, I will not fail you."

"Bonnie, my sweet darling," Anna Beth had cooed seventeen years prior, brushing the tip of her nose against Bonnie's delicious pink button of a nose. Her sweet, newborn smell had filled Anna Beth with hope. "Never before has the Earth welcomed such a beautiful angel. My angel." With one long, slender finger, Anna Beth traced the line of Bonnie's cupid bow and kissed her soft cheeks for the hundredth time that morning.

For seventeen long years stuck between the swamp and bayou, surrounded by the Huet Pointe's cruel nature and the farmers and fishermen and the Leech's criticism, Anna Beth dreamt of Bonnie's debut. Her precious angel was her ticket away from the soggy misery that was Huet Pointe. With the perfect debut Anna Beth intended to bid a delightful farewell to the Leech, Huet Pointe, and the tiny graves of the three stillborn babies and one infant lying just beyond her garden, abandon all as a wealthy widow thankful to live near, or even with, her only child.

"Oh, child," the Leech said to Bonnie, bringing Anna Beth back to the present, "you are the sky reflected on the Gulf in that blue. It's a pity your mother doesn't see that. Do you agree with her choice of white?" Mother McLeary leaned forward, plucking a truffle from the cut crystal bowl on the coffee table. When she bit into it, a bit of ganache dribbled onto her pointed chin. The ganache threatened to drop onto her bodice but clung to a ripple of sagging skin instead.

"Let's not rehash the dress. There's no point in picking." Anna Beth's mother squeezed Bonnie's hand. "You will be a vision in white. And you," she said motioning to the Leech, "have chocolate on your chin." She took a linen napkin from the tray on the coffee table and passed it across Bonnie.

"There is simply no point sharing my wisdom when you two gang up on me." Mother McLeary grabbed the napkin and swiped at the chocolate, smearing it rather than wiping her chin clean.

"We're not ganging up on you," Bonnie said, squeezing Mother McLeary's hand. She took the napkin from Mother McLeary and gently dabbed her Gran Mere's chin until the chocolate residue was gone.

"Not you, pet." Mother McLeary popped another truffle in her mouth, mashing her teeth through the chocolate while glaring at her daughter-in-law.

Anna Beth often pondered how lucky her mother-in-law was to at one time in her life, very early on, find a man to take her in. How did her dead in-laws trick the poor bastard into marrying such a catastrophe? Perhaps she should tiptoe into the pantry late one night, tip back the lid to the chocolate, and then let the little, yellow beads roll from the linen into the jar. But, *no, no, that might harm my exquisite Bonnie as well, even though I have warned her that eventually the chocolates will appear on her hips and belly and bloat her perfect chin.*

"Well, Mother McLeary," Anna Beth said, "I find a casual approach to invitations beyond reproach. Is it so much to ask that *your* people respond in a timely manner?" She paused for a moment waiting for the old woman to respond, knowing she wouldn't dare. "But all is not lost. New Orleans is, after all, only our third choice. We have two coming all the way from Richmond. They will be our main targets. And one family has confirmed from Mobile. If Virginia is lost, Mobile will do."

"But what do we know of any of them?" Bonnie asked her mother. She crinkled her nose as if she detected a stench from states away.

"What we know is that any of these families, the Virginians or Alabamians, will keep you in silk for the rest of your life. And, I'm starting to have my doubts regarding New Orleans and Louisiana as a whole." She couldn't resist digging into the Leech one more time. "That is all that matters." Anna Beth pursed her lips together so not to spit out what actually mattered most was that Virginia, Mobile, even New Orleans, was not Huet Pointe.

"But what if I don't like them? What if they are all fat or ugly or have huge noses that drip and whistle?"

"Bonnie, I will hear none of that." Anna Beth chided her daughter without looking directly at her. Instead, she studied the names on the seating chart. "And, if you are so worried about noses you can see many of them next week at the polo match. I've been told many of the young bachelors will be playing on both sides. Now, no more of that fretting. All this worrying will ruin your digestion and do God knows what to your skin. You must take the upmost care of yourself for the next several weeks. Understood?"

"Yes. Of course. But why not a boy from a family closer to home? To you and Papa? What if I don't want to live all the way in Virginia? I will miss you both dearly. No, I do not want them. You might as well retract the invitation to any of the Virginians straight away."

"Bonnie Eloise McLeary, you will be delightful to each and every one of the young men I have selected for you. You will make them, each one, more enamored than the others. You will not say a word of whether or not any of this displeases you in any way. Do you understand me?"

"Of course, Mother." A pout replaced Bonnie's smile, one that had no effect whatsoever on Anna Beth. Pouting was considered as indolent as mauve in Anna Beth's world.

"Good. Now, leave me. All of you. I feel a headache approaching from all this nattering."

Mother McLeary grabbed another truffle as she, Bonnie, and Anna Beth's mother stood to leave. The rustling skirts and creaking joints and licking of old-lady fingers and smacking of old-lady lips pricked the back of Anna Beth's neck. *At what point,* she thought, *did they turn from Bonnie into the haggard shells before me? How long do I have before I turn that horrible corner?*

"Anna Beth," her mother said, re-entering the room after the Leech and Bonnie had left. "Perhaps you should not force a Richmond proposal on Bonnie."

"I want what is best for her. Richmond is best."

"Is it? How much do you even remember? Maybe you've elevated it in your memory a bit."

"An elevation from this place? Mother, I just couldn't imagine," Anna Beth scoffed.

"Anna Beth, your father and I did the best for you we could. Is your life here really so terrible?"

"Father died. You tried."

"When did you develop such a wicked side?"

"Hah. Good rhyme, Mother. My wicked side, as you say, perhaps arrived as soon as my feet landed on this pungent soil. Or maybe it was when three babies died in my womb? Not even given the chance to breathe this foul air. No, no, Mother. I bet I became so hateful when my little Matthew perished, alone in his bassinette." Anna Beth almost allowed the pain on her lips to extend to fill her eyes with tears. Almost.

"You've suffered much, my love. I will not deny you that. But you must remember all of this is in God's hands. We must be patient and allow God to reveal his will for Bonnie. Do not allow your pain to diminish her. No matter how grand *your* will is." The timeworn woman stood still long enough for her words to resonate in the sudden silence of the parlor. Then, with a swish, swish of her skirts, she left the room. Anna Beth turned from her mother and eyed one of the crystal chachkies perched atop the mantle. Had she thrown it at the back of her mother's head, it would have made a glorious sound.

Anna Beth eyed the truffles, imagining the soft ganache melting on her own tongue, quieting her rage, but thought better of it as her corset tightened around her ribs and dug into her soft belly. Instead, she rose and glided across the parlor then the polished pine floorboards of the hallway, and out the French doors that led to the garden.

The air was thick with the Angel's Trumpet perfume, a heavenly scent Anna Beth could not resist. She bent near the first bush until her nose was just a few inches from a soft, white, open bloom. Once a day, twice on days that jabbed at old wounds, she allowed herself the pleasure of walking through the garden. With much to do in the upcoming weeks, what with Bonnie's debut being a mere six months away, moments to refocus her thoughts were necessary.

As she inhaled, enveloped by the scent, an unexpected touch made her jump, nearly bumping the nearest bloom. When she turned, her husband Gil was before her, his hands reaching for her waist.

"You startled me," she said without leaning into him.

"How long do you plan to admire your flowers today?"

Anna Beth did her best to hide the cringe Gil conjured. "Only a moment more."

"It's Tuesday."

"Yes. Tuesday."

"Will I see you tonight?"

"It is Tuesday," she said, allowing a coy smile to spread across her face.

"My favorite day of the week."

"You've not changed a bit. Twenty years and you still have that itch."

"Yes, and it's really bothering me today. Perhaps my wife could nurse me back to health?" Gil bent and kissed Anna Beth just below her right ear, a display of affection that sent a shudder down her spine. With a boyish grin, Gil walked away, leaving Anna Beth with her flowers.

Anna Beth watched him go then flattened her smile, smoothing the skin near her mouth with her fingers. Turning back to the flowers, she allowed the perfume to settle her mind. An opiate of sorts, the scent calmed her nerves and transported her away from Huet Pointe. She paced the garden until twilight as her mind bounced from golden dust to soiled handkerchiefs, from seating charts to ignored invitations.

She saw the dust cloud first then the coach as it rounded the curve of the driveway.

Tilly hopped from the carriage and hustled to her mistress.

"Did you make the arrangements for the dress?"

Tilly nodded a yes.

"And Mamba Loo? Will she be here in the morning?"

Again, a nod.

"Good. Now, I need to change clothes." Anna Beth pulled a handkerchief from her bodice. With it, she stripped the pollen from a fat anther inside one bell. "Shh," Anna Beth instructed, one finger pressed against her lips. "Our secret," she whispered to Tilly with a slight grin. With the yellow powder collected in the organza-trimmed linen, she headed for the French doors. "You'll need to soak this skirt immediately. Gil was in the swamps. Thoughtless as he is, he grabbed me and smeared that muck all over my skirt. I'm afraid it's already ruined."

Gil, Anna Beth thought, *he refuses to understand.* Of course, she was grateful to him for what he provided. He did agree to the marriage after her father dropped dead one week before her own debut. Her mother, born pathetic in Anna Beth's mind, grieved so that she canceled the affair. Within weeks of the funeral, all of Richmond knew of her father's debts. Every acceptable suitor vanished. She knew why her mother had to seek a match outside of Richmond, but never forgave her for Huet Pointe.

And Anna Beth never forgave Gil either, no matter how lush her garden or full her wardrobe. What art, what culture, what society could a swamp provide her? "Perhaps you should sit by the docks and wait for your precious culture to arrive," Anna Beth's mother had once snapped, shortly after their arrival in Huet Pointe.

"I'd still be sitting there when the rapture comes," Anna Beth had snapped back. With her marriage to Gil came a life of mud-stained hems and pots filled with possum, which had never passed her lips. Over her two decades with Gil, three cooks had tried, and three cooks found themselves back in the sugarcane fields.

Later, Tilly, as she did every Tuesday evening, brought two glasses of brandy to Anna Beth's bedroom. Anna Beth smiled, the silver handle of her hairbrush glittering in the soft light of the oil lamp. The fabric of her white, silk dressing gown flowed loosely away from her bosom and hips and puddled slightly on the floor. The hem was frayed a bit from years of wear, but it was Gil's favorite, so she wore it once weekly to fulfill her wifely duty.

After Tilly left, closing the door without a sound, Anna Beth retrieved a pollen-filled handkerchief from her chifferobe. With delicate fingers she unfolded the cloth and allowed the yellow beads to drop into one glass. With a hairpin, she stirred the brandy until every bit of yellow dust dissolved.

With both glasses, across the hall she went, tapping twice on the door opposite her own.

"Hello, my love," Gil said, opening the door to his bedroom. He looked upon her with more affection than Anna Beth could ever muster for him, even in the early days of their marriage when everything should have been poetic anticipation, foreplay, and climax.

She offered him a brandy.

"You take such good care of me," he told her, taking a sip. He seemed to savor the drink for a moment, swishing the liquid around on his tongue before swallowing.

"I try," she said and watched his larynx move in and out with each sip. *Down the hatch.*

She had considered other options. She could tell him to take his desires two miles down the rutted road that led away from the grand home. Take his sweat and needs to Ruth White's old place. Gil could tell the new head whore all about his needs and wealth and the headaches and desires that come with all his money and leave Anna Beth to her flowers and Bonnie. But Gil would contract syphilis from one of the little whores within minutes. Madness was an unforgiveable sin, at least to Anna Beth. And, she'd still be stuck in Huet Pointe, which was the real, unmanageable problem.

She toyed for a mere minute with the idea of divorce, but that was simply laughable. She in no way could return to Richmond a discarded woman. And Gil would never agree to it. No, divorce is a privilege available only to men.

So, she came to the conclusion that Gil must die, and poison was her best option. Discreet. Clean, for the most part. Practical.

But, which one, which poison should she use? Like a debut, death requires careful thought and preparation, the kind that approaches without detection. The kind that made women whisper, "He was looking a bit pale, but I thought he was just working too hard," and "Poor man. No one knew he was ill."

Hemlock? No. Growing the flowering bush would arouse suspicion and was much better suited for dryer soil rather than the marsh that surrounded her. Any decent gardener knew that.

Belladonna? No. Too hard to come by and Gil hated all berries. Brandy was much more his style.

Cyanide? She needed a slow, believable end to her marriage. Cyanide was far too quick and violent. She'd be hanged before the body soured.

Arsenic? Foolish and bourgeois—two attributes Anna Beth did not possess. Arsenic, although accessible, was too detectable, even that incompetent doctor she blamed for each of her dead babies could have recognized an arsenic poisoning. And what was she supposed to do? Have the porter take her to Hodges so she could place an order? "Five-pound bag of Arsenic, please, Mr. Hodges," she'd say. "And wrap it up nice and tight so none spills as we ride though the craters and muck on our way home." What would she tell the nosy shopkeeper it was for? True, she could claim she needed to poison the gigantic rats that live in the swamp in this god-forsaken sinkhole of a town. But, no, no, no. She had a household staff for poisoning pests, and thankfully, mercifully, blessedly, they were good at their job.

Then, weeks ago, she had remembered her angels and her grandfather. The English style garden tucked behind her grandparents' home in Richmond had been her favorite fantasyland as a child. The aroma altered from bush to flowering bush with lavender and basil and mint mixing with the lilies and roses and her favorite, the Angel's Trumpet.

"Don't get too close," her grandfather warned one afternoon as a ten-year-old Anna Beth leaned in to bathe in the perfume. "A little of that and you'll lose your senses. Too much will make you lose your bowels." Grandfather chuckled afterward as Anna Beth feigned objection to such talk.

"That pretty plant helped us win the war," Grandfather told Anna Beth. According to legend, a group of British soldiers were poisoned with Angel's Trumpet pollen one chilly, fall night. They lost their minds and bowels. Many lost their lives during the one-sided battle that followed the toxic plot. Ten-year-old Anna Beth was hooked, and Grandfather gave the girl her first Angel's Trumpet clipping that day.

So, Anna Beth had turned to her favorite flower just as those brave, cunning patriots had so many decades before. She began to add a bit of pollen to Gil's brandy every Tuesday. He would surely begin to show signs of madness first, bothersome but short-lived and followed by intestinal distress. Week after week, the symptoms would increase as the dose increased. The staff may worry for their master, but none would know the root cause. By the time the deed was done, the Angel's Trumpet would be dormant for winter, and the twit and twaddle of Huet Pointe ignorant as always.

In Gil's bedroom, Anna Beth finished her brandy, gulping the last swallow so as to hurry the evening along. She stepped out of her dressing gown, not bothering to pick it up from the floor.

As she lay on her back, with Gil rubbing and pressing and doing all the things he thought made him a good man and husband, Anna Beth closed her eyes and thought of scents. Beef roast braising on a stove in Richmond, waiting to be devoured by a happily fat and wrinkled widow. The sweet hairline of Bonnie's first child, once she became wife and mother. The oil lamps of Richmond's Grand Theatre as the first notes of the overture play. Angel's Trumpet offering a soft "Good evening, Ma'am." Chocolate dripping down her chin. Death.

"Brandy again next Tuesday?" Anna Beth asked as she dressed afterward, securing the last button of her gown.

"Of course, my love," Gil answered.

"Happily then. Sleep well, dear."

🎺

Ernestine

ERNESTINE HARRIS REJECTED many of the matronly activities of Huet Pointe. She had no use for planning parties, needlepoint, or gumbo recipes. She had no daughters in need of grooming, only sons who inherited their father's stunning green eyes and sullen neglect, the ability to privilege work over her needs without a tinge of guilt. To her mind, complicated dinner parties, debutantes, or the perfect alternating continental stitch improved Huet Pointe in no meaningful way. Rather early in her life as Madam Dr. Walter Harris, Ernestine chose to pass her minutes, hours, and days in a more altruistic activity. She tended her roses.

As a young mother, the wife of Huet Pointe's first official doctor had lined the front walk of her modest foursquare, Main Street home with blood red roses. She found the contrast to the white clapboard satisfying. If a better color existed to highlight a home built on broken bones, lacerations, bloodletting, and childbirth, she didn't know one.

Decades later, she considered her roses a source of pride for all who called Huet Pointe home. Why else did so many linger in front of her home, slowing to a crawl as they passed the fifty-foot stretch of thick green shrubs ablaze in red blooms?

Ernestine considered her green thumb a divine gift. If not for her predictable roses and her ability to care for them, her husband's erratic schedule would have done her in—withered on the vine, perished of drought. The midnight knocks on the front door for a baby with croup. A woman in labor, one in which the midwife had lost control. Yellow fever unknowingly brought to town on the wings of mosquitos. Walter even tended to a ship of tubercular pirates, braving the quarantined, putrid throng to offer what comfort he could. That particular peril—a rather selfish one if he'd bothered to ask Ernestine–had been nearly in vain as he was one of the only survivors. But how his stock went up in the chitter-chatter circles of Huet Pointe!

Yes, Ernestine's Walter was damn near sainthood, she knew. So, she accepted the interrupted dinners, waking up alone, and rearing her three boys with little more than a passing glance from her dear, devoted doctor-husband. This was her cross in life, but even the heaviest of crosses could have order and beauty if she made it so. So, season after season, year after year, she tended her roses.

If cared for with devotion, roses are predictable. A fussy perennial, the buds will return. Each fall, Ernestine thought the anticipation would torture her into an early grave, teased for days by clinched buds. Then in a glorious, stupendous act of God Almighty, the roses burst open. *Hello, world!* For the sake of that delectable moment, Ernestine never neglected the pruning for fear that the thorny stems tangle and fail to produce new buds. If she forgot to water the dark green shrubs for even one day, the blooms withered, blood red fading to something akin to iron deficiency. If overly zealous with water, the roots rotted.

"No one likes wet feet," Ernestine had told Miss Ellie Weaver one afternoon as Ellie allowed her dog to sniff around the roses. Bending to dispense a single cupful of water on the next bush, Ernestine flared her nostrils. "Please do not allow that creature to relieve himself on my roses."

Ellie, ten or twelve—Ernestine neither knew nor cared about the girl's exact age—at the time, responded. "*That creature* has a name. Sterling. His name is Sterling."

"What a ridiculous name for a mutt. There's nothing sterling about him."

And so began the near decade-long feud, Ellie Weaver and her dog versus Ernestine Harris and her roses.

"Miss Weaver," Ernestine said, many years after her first encounter with the young lady's pooch. "Your dog has been at my roses again." Ernestine stood bent with her nose two inches from a leaf as Ellie hustled toward the rose bushes and Sterling, a petite terrier with an impatient bladder.

Ernestine pinched one arm of her spectacles in front of the leaf to magnify the tiny, black spot. "That. That is what I want you to see. Again. That black spot!" Even though a mere two millimeters wide, the spot bore the weight of the Original Sin, at the very least the mark of Cain. God himself challenged Ernestine with the mark. She would not fail Him.

Across the street, two housemaids, Mamba Loo, house slave of the Durand Plantation, and Sabine Fredieu, the Lawry's beck-and-call girl, paused their walk to Hodges General Store, hopeful to witness another of Ernestine and Ellie's classic dog-piss-rose-spot exchanges. If so, they would be the hit of the bonfire that evening.

"Hmm-hmm. Them white women bought to go at it again," Mamba Loo whispered under her breath.

Sabine tried to flatten a smile, but the corners of her mouth curled as she gently tugged on Mamba Loo's arm. "Slow up a bit. See what the crazy old bat has for Miss Ellie today."

"You know she gonna be hemmin' and hawin' over spots or such. Too bad her ol' man ain't well enough to check her eye's." Mamba Loo let out a snicker. "Them specs ain't doing no good."

"I don't think the problem is with her eyes," Sabine said.

Ernestine faced the canine perpetrator's keeper, using her spectacles as a schoolmarm's pointer. "Do you know what black spots on rose bushes are caused by?"

"I'm sure you will inform me as you've informed me before," Ellie said, smiling at the tiny terrier dipping his nose beneath her hem.

"Do not use that tone with me, young lady. Just because your Daddy is dead, does not mean you've no one to answer to."

"Oh, Lord, Miz Ernestine done brought the dead daddy into it." Mamba Loo cut a glance to Sabine; one that said *this is going to be a good one.*

"If you'd known my father as you claim to, you would know he raised me to be kind and reverent. I never disrespect my *elders.* Perhaps you need to lay down. The summer air seems to have lingered this year. Maybe that's what's caused the spots."

"Miss Weaver, calling me old is of no consequence. Every morning that I wake up a day older is a blessed victory in the Lord." Ernestine pointed again to the spot. "This black spot is the result of that creature urinating on my roses. Little drops seep into the leaves, poisoning them. Do you see? Here and here."

"Yes, ma'am, I see them. But how do you know my Sterling is responsible? As I've told you before, any number of creatures or natural occurrences could cause those spots. I deal with them in my own garden."

"How dare you compare those weeds you grow to my prize roses?"

"Oh, now that's just mean. I've seen Miss Ellie's garden. It's lovely," Sabine said.

"I think that was her point. She know ain't nobody gonna call her out for actin' a fool. Hell's bells, that's what I'm lookin' to do most when I get to Miss Ernestine's age— act a fool all day and all night." Mamba Loo shuffled her feet a bit as if possessed by a jig.

"Perhaps yesterday's rain is the culprit." Ellie reached in the ample pocket of her apron and retrieved a small, white biscuit. Sterling hopped in circles until at last Ellie dropped the treat in the grass. Sterling pounced, gobbling up the biscuit.

"Rainwater never dries on my roses. I don't allow it. Why do you think I'm out here after every shower shaking each stem?"

"Because she ain't got the sense God gave a goat," Mamba Loo said, a bit louder than she should have. Then, she let out a holler of a laugh.

"You two best get on now before I get the Sheriff," Ernestine snapped, glaring at the gawking women until they scurried away. Then, as red-faced as her roses, she turned back to Ellie. "I know you've seen me out here after the rain. I see you peek through those heavy drapes of yours. I see you. You watch that vermin leave your yard, cross the street, and lift her leg. Every morning and every night, pissing on my roses."

"How dare you sit in judgment of me whilst saying such things?" Ellie bent down and snatched the pooch from the ground. "Come, Sterling, let's not endure Miss Harris's vulgarity any longer."

"Do not let me catch that thing near my property again!"

Later that evening, Ernestine lay in wait beyond a streaked parlor window. As soon as Sterling crossed the street for his evening release and headed toward the third rosebush on the left, Ernestine sprang from her chair, through the door, and onto the porch. Armed with a broom in one hand and a rolled newspaper in the other, she lumbered down her porch stairs. A muscle in her back twisted so that she screamed. Or maybe yelped. Or hollered as loud as Mamba had laughed earlier that day. The sound made no difference other than doing the job intended for the paper and broom. Sterling turned, his weak bladder leaking onto his fur as he scurried away.

At first light, Ernestine woke and dressed in the converted dining room, careful to step only on the floorboards that resisted creaking. What used to house family dinners with her three boys now served as her bedroom, the stairs too steep for her old bones to reach the master bedroom. She chose her most severe navy, high-collar blouse, and skirt for the business of the day. Only one petticoat should make her walk easier. Two additional hairpins secured her hat just in case the bayou winds were churning, signaling winter's imminent approach.

As she checked her reflection in the mirror, the sun cast its first of many rays through a slit in the curtain, illuminating the china hutch. It being too cumbersome to move from the dining room when her boys, now men with busy lives, moved Ernestine and Walter's bed, armoires, and vanity downstairs, the hutch remained against the wall opposite the four-poster bed. The light bounced off the gold leaf of a dinner plate as if to wish her well in her endeavors.

The house wept with neglect as Ernestine crossed from the dining room through the parlor. It begged for a good dusting with each creak of the floor. The silver picture frames had long given up on being polished. The flat expressions of their inhabitants—Ernestine and Walter on their wedding day, Ernestine with each of the boys following a generous dousing with Holy Water during their christenings—revealed their disappointment with their current living conditions, as did the chandelier in the foyer. Had Ernestine the physical capability of lighting any of the candles ensconced in the crystal, molded petal cups, the house would burn to the ground, fire fueled by a collection of dust and debris. But, alas, her bones were too old and tired to fight cobwebs and dust bunnies, and her Walter had lost the ability to fight at all.

In the parlor, a cockeyed tower of novels stood, their covers unopened, given to her by well-meaning but grossly uninformed daughters-in-law. The sewing basket of batiste handkerchiefs endured the same cruel fate, death by deterioration under a thick coating of filth. Not a single stitch of a monogram had been attempted.

On the porch, she pulled the front door tight behind her, tugging until the click signaled that all was secure. She reached up and straightened the fading shingle hanging from the right column—*The Doctor is out.* Then, with one hand on the railing, she descended the stairs and walked downtown.

As the bells of Our Lady of Sorrow chimed the eighth final ring of the hour, Ernestine huffed up the three steps to Sheriff Tuckey's office. The portly man gulped the last of his morning coffee when Ernestine pushed the door open.

"Tuckey, I demand you do something about that dog!"

"Well, good morning to you too, Miz Harris."

"It will be if you agree to get off your lazy hind quarters and fix that dog."

"And what poor creature has got you in such a tizzy?" Tuckey sat up in his chair, leaning on his ample elbows for support.

"You know perfectly well I am speaking of Ellie Weaver's runt of a dog."

"Pissin' on your tulips again, huh?"

"Roses. That dog is killing my roses. Now, do I need to remind you that my roses increase the value of every property in Huet Pointe?"

"You may need to explain to me why you think a few shrubs affect property values. And, while you're here, explain to me how controlling the animal population of this town falls under my jurisdiction. No flower's gonna up the price of sugarcane and no sheriff spends his day chasing puppies."

"She is trespassing on my property." Ernestine, too angry to sit, stood before Tuckey glaring at him the same way she did Mamba Loo and Sabine the day before. To her dismay, Tuckey appeared unmoved.

"Ellie Weaver is trespassing on your property?" Tuckey asked.

"Not Miss Weaver. The mutt."

"Dogs don't trespass. They just go."

"That dog trots over to my yard every evening, as if invited by the Heavenly Father, even though I've told Miss Weaver to keep her out. She sniffs around the third bush on the right, then relieves herself right there in front of me and God and everybody."

"As I have told you before, and if there is a God in Heaven this will be the last time I have to tell you, that dog has decided that your roses are her spot. She marked it. That's nature. Ain't nothing I can do about nature."

Ernestine huffed again, exacerbated by Tuckey's repeated suggestion that the dog's actions are natural and her roses will just be the damned thing's victims. "So, I am just supposed to do nothing and wait for the nuisance to die?"

"Perhaps you should go across the street and light a candle for an early demise. Put an extra coin in the pot for good favor and quick action."

"Sheriff, that is near blasphemous!"

"It's the only course of action you got."

Ernestine considered a stroll to the church for a second then dismissed the thought. Praying for death seemed sinful. However, the dog being dead would be ideal.

"Thank you, Sheriff Tuckey. As usual, you've been fully and utterly useless." Ernestine turned on her heels and yanked the door open causing that same fussy muscle in her back to cry a bit.

Under the morning sun, she imagined for the thousandth time a world without Sterling: Bright red roses absent of spots. She could gaze upon them from her silent front porch freed of Sterling's yapping and panting. But could she ask God to do what she was unwilling to do herself? Would merely praying fulfill her gift of freewill? If capable and for the greater good, which all knew her roses were, shouldn't she perform the deed?

Her brain flooded with possible ways to eliminate a pest—rat poisoning, shovel to the skull, a trap. And what, pray tell, should she do with the carcass? Scoop the bloody thing up with the same shovel and deposit it on Ellie's yard? Take it to Hodges to have it ground into fertilizer? Bury it by the magnolia tree in the back yard? She simply couldn't dig a sufficient hole, not with her back screaming at her.

Three doors down, Ernestine stomped into Hodges General Store. On her way to the counter, Ernestine eyed a roll of chicken wire. For half a second, she considered trapping Sterling, but then thought better of it. Once she caged the animal, she'd no idea what to do with it. No idea until she, while waiting for Mr. Hodges to finish with the McLeary's mute housekeeper, eyed that week's newspaper. The headline told a grisly tale of a local, legendary alligator and the latest Huet Pointe resident to fall victim to his ferocious appetite and death spiral.

"What can I do you for, Miz Harris?" Mr. Hodges asked from behind the counter.

"First, I was wondering if my fertilizer was in yet? It's been two weeks now."

"Should be a couple more days. The shipment was delayed. Coach got caught up in some mess in Mobile."

"Oh. Well. Well, then, please put a bag of flour and can of lard on my tab. I have a sudden craving for biscuits."

"Um, certainly." Mr. Hodges hesitated. "Your tab—"

"My youngest should be around in a few weeks to settle up with you." Ernestine glared at Mr. Hodges ready to remind him of all the midnight emergencies he had called upon her husband to solve. His three girls, one after the other like steps, seemed to invite trouble, freak accidents, and bacteria.

"And how are your boys? I hadn't seen 'em around much last year or so," Hodges inquired.

"Thomas and Robert are both doctors now, so their patients keep them quite busy. Lewis is an attorney over in New Orleans. Trying to keep those Cajun crooks straight. He should be over for a visit soon."

"I'm not surprised to hear of their success, what with them being so smart and Walter as an example."

"Of course. Walter." Ernestine glanced at her watch, eager to get home.

Hodges got the hint, being far from stupid himself. "Here you go." Mr. Hodges handed Ernestine a white cotton sack with flour and lard.

Later that evening, after a light supper of freshly baked biscuits and milk, Ernestine dropped one fat crumb then another and another on the ground until she had formed a trail of Sterling-sized biscuit bites from the third rosebush on the left to behind her house.

At approximately eight in the evening, as the last of the mosquitoes bid her goodnight, Ernestine sat in the white, wooden swing-for-two hung between two columns of the back porch, a tea towel over her skirted lap. As if on cue, Sterling trotted around the corner of the house, enticed by the biscuit crumbs. From the swing, Ernestine extended her arm toward the dog and opened her palm. A biscuit lay in her hand. She held it out of Sterling's reach until the morsel of a pooch jumped into Ernestine's lap and licked the crumbs from her fingers. Biscuit crumbs cascaded from Sterling's happy jaws to the tea towel.

Ernestine swaddled Sterling in the towel and stood. She held the dog tight to her body as she walked the wooded path that led from her back yard to the bayou. The dog let out a few muffled yelps, but none loud enough to draw attention.

At 9:30 pm, as she did every night, Ernestine pulled a crisp white sheet across her nightgown and bare ankles then unfolded the day-old newspaper. In the lamplight, Ernestine surveyed the headlines.

"Walter, look at this. Tarasque has been at it again. Apparently, this time he ate some poor prostitute. Ruth White. Well, one less of her kind is not such a bad thing." Ernestine pointed at the headline, turning the paper so Walter, lying in his permanent spot, could see the sketch of the legendary alligator.

"You're late," Walter mumbled in a language only Ernestine could understand. The massive stroke he'd suffered the previous spring had left his left leg and arm useless, his right side terribly weak, and had mangled his tongue. What syllables he could form were pushed through uncooperative lips.

"I know, my darling. I'm so sorry. I had pressing business to attend to." Ernestine reached over and pulled Harold's blanket up under his chin.

Harold attempted a confused look coupled with more mumbling.

"No, no. Nothing for you to worry about. I took care of it. Now, back to Tarasque." As she leaned back to entertain Walter with stories of gators and the frivolities of Huet Pointe's wanting social scene, Walter's green eyes, the one part of his body unchanged by the stoke, smiled at her. *Still the healer*, she thought, as the fretful muscle in her back began to loosen.

The next morning, as Ernestine gave each of her rosebushes its morning cup of water, Ellie Weaver ran to her from across the street.

"Have you seen Sterling? He's missing." Ellie's nose and eyes were red.

"No, I haven't seen him today, come to think of it." Ernestine gave Ellie little notice as she moved to the next rosebush.

"I'm beside myself with worry. I haven't seen him since last night."

"Do you think he's run off?"

"He wouldn't do that. I'm all he knows."

"Well," Ernestine said, dropping the ladle in the nearly empty bucket and rising to meet Ellie's troubled gaze, "According to the paper, Tarasque has been at it again. You may want to check down by the shore. But don't go alone. You never know where that beast may be hiding."

Ellie cupped her hand over her mouth, stifling a cry.

❦

Part Three: Winter

Coraline

CORALINE DURAND SAW THE DEVIL. She knew his face.

Was her bogeyman out among the trees and moss, lurking down by the creek, slithering around some stump in the swamp? No. The trees and moss and water and critters had nothing to do with what her devil did. The devil Coraline knew killed her Mama. Her devil made her an orphan, a thing to be pitied. In return, Coraline's heart ordered a reckoning.

Reckonings require planning, calculation, manipulation. Coraline was capable of all, but sometimes tripped over her youth as she did on the night she misjudged a neglected board in the footbridge, slipped on building frost, and tore her knee from here to Betsy on a stray nail. As soon as she felt the nail slice a gaping hole in her stockings and rip her soft skin, she knew she was done for.

If Mamba Loo saw her scraped knee and ripped flannel stockings, Coraline would have to confess her late-night reconnaissance. She'd tried to lie to Mamba before, after she'd climbed to the top of her armoire, grabbed hold of the drapes, and leapt. She swung clear across the expanse of the double windows, but the death-defying feat brought down the drapes, upholstery rod and all. Coraline landed with a thud, as did the heavy rod. She had popped up and scrambled to the nook opposite the ruined wall.

Crouching in front of her pristine dollhouse, Coraline pretended to play as Mamba Loo rushed into the room. Coraline had turned, looked Mamba Loo straight in the eyes and lied. "I've no idea what brought those drapes down. Maybe you didn't hang them right after cleaning them. That's right dangerous."

Mamba Loo towered over her and sniffed the air above Coraline's head. "There's a stench about you, child. This whole room stinks of your lies." For three days and three nights whenever Mamba Loo and Coraline were in the same room together, which was quite often, Mamba Loo had complained of the smell.

So, lying was out of the question. Coraline would have to come clean with Mamba Loo. But maybe she could convince Mamba not to tell Grandmama.

Grandmama was a different set of troubles. Coraline knew that scene. Every moment played out in her mind. The old black woman stands before the old white woman—two halves of a black and white cookie shaking their heads in disbelief. Next, Grandmama dismisses Mamba Loo while lamenting on what to "do about that child!" But Coraline knew exactly what Grandmama would do. That old woman with her proper, well-bred coating and mean as tar filling knew of only one way to deal with wild children. Grab a switch, a bare bottom, and whip the wild out.

Blasted frost! I should've known the boards would be slick. Coraline smacked the thick blankets and sheets. *Eleven years old is far too old to be put over someone's knee!*

Lying flat on her back, she stared at the ceiling and felt her knee pulse. Up until that mistake, Coraline had been so careful, methodical, like the squirrel that lived in Coraline's escape route. She'd studied his every move from the moment he'd peek out of his nest to then jump one, two, three branches down. With his tail tucked low, he'd scurry down the trunk. On the ground, he'd tilt his face to the sky, two sniffs for targets and a third for the hawk. Then, when the coast was surely clear, he'd dash to the pecan trees. Over and over and over, that squirrel never faltered. The squirrel never slipped on a slick root, dragging his knee across a nail.

"Coraline Durand! You best be out that bed."

Hellfire and damnation! Coraline enjoyed the adult words she heard around the plantation and often whispered the naughty words when she was alone. Once she even heard Grandmama swear, but that wrinkled bag of hypocrisy denied it when Coraline pressed her on the matter. *Someone should put that old bag of bones over their knee – once for swearing then again for stinking up the place with her lies.*

Coraline hopped out of bed, wincing as her nightgown brushed against her knee. Like the squirrel, she'd taken the tree trunk as a ladder, dashed through the woods, across the creek, through the sugarcane field, and finally swung one leg then the other over the low-hanging branch of her spying spot, an ancient oak whose roots stretched all the way to her devil's massive plantation home. From that spot, she had done what she did at least twice a week: She tracked the murderer's movements and planned her reckoning.

"You best be up and ready to dress!" The flat-nosed Mamba Loo flung the door open, barely looking at the girl as she burst through the door, her black-as-night arms full of woolen sleeves and skirts of pale blue and white petticoats.

Coraline frowned at the ruffled pantaloons peeking from the bottom of the pile. The ruffles of eyelet lace began at the knees and fell one after another down to the ankle. "Morning, Mamba," Coraline said. "Why is it that I have to knock on every door in this house, but you and Grandmama don't?"

"You startin' in on the sass early this morning, child. Good thing your grandma drags your behind to church. You surely needs it. Now, off with that gown. We gotta wash up."

"I can do it myself."

"Oh, you think you's grown and needs privacy, do you? Well, you ain't grown and until you can handle all these bows and buttons Miz Durand insists on, you ain't doing nothing yourself."

Coraline turned her back to Mammie and pulled her white, cotton nightgown over her head. What used to be flat had begun to round and swell, but in that moment, Coraline's worry wasn't about her growing breasts.

"Now, why you being so shy, child? Turn 'round." Mamba Loo spun Coraline by the shoulders. Her eyes spread like hotcakes on a cast iron skillet. "Coraline Bissett Durand, what happened to your knee?"

"I...I...um..."

"What on earth caused such a..." She dropped her volume to a whisper. "You snuck out of this house last night, didn't you? Took it 'pon yourself to slide out your warm bed, slip through that there window, and shimmy down that tree. Didn't you? Didn't you?"

"Yes, Mammie, but I—Wait. How do you know that?"

"Never you mind how I know. You just mind *that* I know. You snuck over to the McLeary's again, ain't you?" Mammie's knees crunched as she stooped to examine the wound.

"What do you mean again? Have you been following me?"

Mamba Loo blew a gentle breeze on the cut. "You snuck out and got yourself hurt and thought nobody'd know. How'd you do it?" Mamba Loo stood and crossed to the basin. She twisted a rag in the cool water. No matter how Mamba Loo's body sagged in places and ballooned in others, her hands resembled a horse's knees, dark and muscular with sharp-angled knuckles.

"You already know the answer to that. I climbed down the tree." Coraline stood naked in the chilly, vast bedroom.

"You are testing me, child. How you get that scrape?" Mamba Loo pressed the cool rag against Coraline's knee. "Now, don't you start flinchin'. You did this to yo'self."

Coraline winced at the rag against her knee. "The footbridge. It was slippery last night."

"Yes, it was. You coulda fell and caught your death in that cold last night. I bet that water is freezin' cold. Cold and dark."

"Well, if you knew I was out, why didn't you stop me?" Tears began to fill the girl's eyes.

"Child, I can't change what's in your heart as much as I can change the weather. You bound and determined to get that man. And when you do, what you plan to do? And, if you go and get yourself caught, what you gonna tell your grandma?"

"Grandmama doesn't want me to go because she doesn't believe me. She thinks I'm lying about what I saw. I'm telling you I saw what I saw!"

Mamba Loo saw the girl's pain every time she looked in her eyes, when the pale green flashed to emerald at the mention of her devil, Mr. Gil McLeary. That pain reached out to Mamba Loo, threatened to wrap its steel hand around her heart, squeeze as if to burst a melon.

With her back to the girl, Mamba Loo dug through the armoire. "Here," she said, turning to face the girl, towering over her, "Put these stockings on so your Grandma don't catch wise to your knee. I'll fix a salve later. Maybe you don't get no infection."

"You're not going to tell?"

"You gonna do this again?"

"Mamba, he has to pay for what he did."

"You still ain't told Mamba what you plan to do. Why you goin' there and spyin' on that man."

"Accidents happen." Coraline stared at Mamba Loo. She breathed in and out, slow and even, as she imagined the fire creeping up the tall white columns and around the verandas. But Coraline couldn't act until the McLeary's daughter was away. Her survival, her being orphaned was part of the reckoning. Bonnie McLeary with all her light and grace and sweetness and cloying perfection needed to know Coraline's pain. It was too big not to share.

"No." Mamba Loo grabbed the girl and pulled her into her bosom. "Baby girl, you still got good in you. You do somethin' to those people and all that good will disappear. I know you hurt. I hurt, too, but you too young to know that kind of satisfaction. Ain't nothing satisfying 'bout carrying guilt and worry." Mamba's blouse dampened with Coraline's tears.

"Just skip to the end when you tell me there ain't nothin' to do about it?"

"Will you listen this time if I do?"

Coraline clamped her lips shut, shaking. Four years of grief took hold of her body.

"I didn't think so." Mamba Loo gently rubbed the girl's back, brushing her large hand in small circles until the shaking subsided. "Now, if I gotta sleep on your floor every night to make sure you ain't sneakin' off, you know I'll do it." Mamba Loo stood Coraline up. One by one she buttoned the wool flannel bodice closed as if her fingers we twenty years younger than the rest of her body. "And know this, for nearly a year now I been following you two times a week. You ain't as sneaky as you think." She gave the girl a final once-over. "Well, Miss Coraline, you may be twisted as a thicket, but you do make a pretty picture." She placed a bonnet on her head, tucked in a stray blonde curl, and tied the scarves into a large bow below the girl's chin. "Soon, your grandma will realize you're getting too old for these little girl things. Believe your old Mamba."

Coraline squeezed Mamba Loo's hand. The cushioned pads and callouses, thick fingers and leathery skin steadied her. "Can't you come with me? Maybe if I asked Grandmama, you could stand in the back with the other nannies."

"Honey, you know that ain't gonna happen. Anyways, I got my own flock to attend."

"So, I'll go with you. Listen to you sing. Watch you dance. 'Least your church makes things happen."

"Now don't you go tellin' folks you know what goes on down there! These white folks'll loose their minds if they think I'm teaching you that. You get ol' Mamba killed. Then who'll make sure you ain't goin' off doing somethin' stupid? You best get on downstairs. I'm sure Miz Durand's been runnin' a hole in the floor worrying that y'all be late."

Coraline turned to go but stopped at the closed door. "Mamba, you know I can't stop until he pays for what he did to Mama. And, to Jojo."

"What you say, child?" Mamba Loo's chest ached at the mention of the name, two syllables she hadn't allowed in nearly four years.

"If you won't do right by your son, I will."

Coraline squared her shoulders and left the bedroom, closing the door behind her. Later, kneeling in the third row of Our Lady of Sorrow, she folded her hands in prayer, kneeling next to her grandmother. The priest droned through the Latin consecration, as the congregation's minds wandered to chores, whether or not the fish would bite in the cool waters, or if anyone would ever invent a more comfortable corset. Coraline, however, had no time for daydreaming. She needed God to grant her wish, Mamba Loo's too, although she'd never given Coraline her consent. *Lord, please help me. Help us, me and Mamba. She deserves justice, too.*

While Coraline prayed to Jesus and Mary and all the Saints in the white church, second largest building in all of Huet Pointe, Mamba Loo sat on the edge of the girl's bed, praying to her own spirits for guidance. She wondered how many others in Huet Pointe knew that when Gil McLeary strung up Jojo, the weakest of the McLeary farmhands, that devil had strung up her baby boy. Did they know that the man they allowed to swing for three full days was innocent? Did they care to know he died for the same reason Coraline's mother did—sugarcane and more room to grow it? Carrying what felt to be all the troubles of the world, Mamba Loo stood and breathed out the answer. *No. And no one ever will.*

***

With the moon high above, Coraline ignored Mamba and all her warnings and shimmied down the tree. Twenty minutes later, she crouched in her spying spot. Her knee stuck to the cotton of her stolen britches thanks to a thick slathering of Mamba Loo's salve. As she picked the fabric, a dark figure, wrapped in a blanket with a tignon wrapped around her head, broke from the tree line and scampered to the stables. Coraline squinted, trying to make out the figure's shape.

***

Seven-year-old Coraline Durand had awakened near midnight on April 2, 1846. An argument boomed from the parlor below her bedroom. She crept to the second-story landing and peered down to see Gil McLeary standing over her mother. Coraline's eyes traveled from Mr. McLeary's boots across her mother's motionless body to the pool of blood surrounding her blonde hair. She cupped her hand over her mouth to stifle the scream.

On April 3, 1846, a gunnysack of silver bobbles belonging to the Durand household was found by one Gil McLeary in the shack of his slave Jojo. At approximately nine that evening, after a quick judgment of guilty on burglary and murder charges was rendered, the McLeary foreman slipped a noose around Jojo's neck and three men heaved until Jojo's legs stopped twitching.

On April 4, 1846, Coraline's grandparents, parents to Jacob Durand, took possession of the Durand land, house, child, and slaves, being the rightful owners of all after the unfortunate but accidental death of their son two years prior and then the murder of their daughter-in-law. As a measure of thanks to Gil McLeary for bringing the killer to such swift justice, Jacob Durand, Sr., deeded forty acres of rich, black soil to Gil McLeary.

After a Sunday morning in early December, 1850, spent praying on the edge of a child's bed, Mamba Loo could ignore her heart no more. The pieces seemed to reassemble and shatter again and again with every passing minute. That night, after tucking Coraline into bed, even though she knew the girl had no intention of sleeping, she slipped out the servants' entrance with a small, flat, metal disc in her hand. She walked the path from the Durand plantation to the McLeary's as if in full daylight, stepping lightly over bulbous tree roots and slick, dewy stones.

The following morning, while on his morning ride, Gil McLeary loaded his musket and searched the tree line for signs of wild turkeys. With the first flutter of dark feathers, Gil McLeary raised the musket, took aim, and fired. A metal disc deep in the barrel blocked the trajectory of the bullet. The explosion was reported to be so fierce that Mr. McLeary's porter was thrown flat on his back. Mr. Gil McLeary blew from his saddle to the ground, his head split wide open against a rock.

***

As Monday morning peeked through Coraline's heavy drapes, she woke to Mamba Loo seated at the foot of her bed.

"You was out late last night," Mamba Loo told her.

"So were you."

Mamba Loo grabbed the child's hand, squeezed, and kissed it. "You don't need to go there no more, baby girl. That devil is done."

❄

Ernestine and Rosarie

ERNESTINE HARRIS SAT STRAIGHT UP in bed at the first knock on her door, always a light sleeper, but cursedly so now that her Walter was bedridden. The hushed but frenetic tapping was all she needed to wake. As her tired eyes tried to adjust to the darkness, the tapping started again.

In only her nightgown, she scurried across the icy floor. Just the first week of January, the almanac rang true. This was to be a colder, wetter, nastier winter for the residents of Huet Pointe than any before it.

"Stop that!" Ernestine said as she yanked the door open. "Rosarie Hodges, you best be dead or dying to knock on my door at this hour."

"I think I used too much." Rosarie's eyes darted from Ernestine to the home next door, the home she shared with Mr. Hodges.

"Too much what?" Ernestine asked. With her adrenaline pumping and cold wind slapping her face she struggled to make sense of Rosarie's panic.

"The powder. The *powder*," Rosarie whisper-yelled. "I think I used too much and now he's…he's…"

"Oh. Well," Ernestine said, and, "Without a thank you note I wasn't sure you received the basket of goodies." Ernestine grabbed her velvet-backed cape from a hook near the door and slipped on a pair of Walter's old boots. The two-size-too-big boots had sat next to the door for nearly a year as if Walter might spring from his bed one day and walk again. Like Ernestine's ever-blooming roses, her hope never withered.

Ernestine stood before Rosarie standing in the doorway. "Are you going to move so an old lady can get by?"

"Where are you going?" Rosarie asked.

Ernestine stomped down the front stairs and through the frost-covered grass. "I'm gonna see what you did. Isn't that why you're pounding on my door?"

"What I did? You gave me the powder! And that note. I had to burn it so Mister Hodges wouldn't see how vulgar you are!"

"Well, that's a fine thing to say considering I'm not," Ernestine paused to climb Rosarie's porch steps, "the one who sprinkled that stuff in my husband's trousers."

Ernestine flung Rosarie's door open to view the scene. One seeming vase in big shards on the floor; its contents scattered. Two overturned chairs. One needlepoint basket resting on its side. One Mr. Hodges with his trousers around his ankles and bare buttocks shining in the moonlight writhing on the floor.

"Good God, Rosarie. How much did you use?"

"The bottle."

"The whole bottle?"

"Yes." Rosarie fell to her knees next to her husband. "Have I ruined him?"

Ernestine squatted on aging knees and tried to look between Mr. Hodges hipbone and the floor. "Hard to tell from this angle. I'm guessing the tender spots are more toward the front."

***

Rosarie Hodges was new to sabotaging her husband's nether regions. Before she'd found the end of her wits and the courage to take action, she appeared perfect. She spoke in a soft, sweet, tone. She walked so that Mr. Hodges never heard the clanking of her boot heels against the hardwood floors. She prepared every meal the man ate. She followed his every instruction when assisting him in his store. And then there was that decade-long arrangement she orchestrated with Ruth White. Although sinful, Rosarie justified her arrangement with Huet Pointe's top whore as a way to provide comfort to her husband—the kind she couldn't. But Ruth White was dead. Any bits of her left behind by Tarasque, the legendary alligator, surely had decomposed—fish food. Ruth White's untimely death left a void in Mr. Hodges' life that Rosarie could not fill with soft footsteps, sweet words, or hot meals.

As the trees lost their dark green leaves, Mr. Hodges grew restless. When the trees stretched out their barren branches in desperate protest against the wet wind, his restlessness turned to anger.

As December approached, vines retreated, shriveling in the cold, refusing to climb until warmer weather returned. The water retreated too, taking with it the fish and crab, forcing fishermen to deeper waters farther from the shore. As the water level sank and the trees grew angry and the vines hid, Rosarie receded, losing her ability to feign any sort of lightness as she did in warmer months. Without feigned buoyancy, she was left with the truth, cold and harsh.

***

Also carried on the wicked December wind, was Huet Pointe's first frost of the season and a severe threat Ernestine Harris heeded. Her precious roses, her babies, were surely the targets of the wind's cruel chill. She knew the wind's intention: to spread icy tentacles around each stem and squeeze until all that remained were mushy, flaccid twigs.

"Yoo-hoo, Miss Ernestine," Rosarie Hodges said one December morning from beyond the right hedge of Ernestine's front yard. "Need help?"

"Yes, please!" Ernestine said, clutching a tarp and fighting the wind as one corner flipped up and smacked Ernestine on the cheek. For several minutes she had tried in vain to cover the first of two dozen rose bushes in need of protection. Behind her on the front steps lay a thigh-high stack of tarps, dingy and threadbare in spots from decades of use. "Grab the other end of this thing so it won't fly up again."

"Of course, of course," Rosarie called. She scurried past the hedgerow to the street then along another row of roses, finally turning into her neighbor's yard between two bushes covered in blood red blooms. "I cannot believe your roses are still blooming."

"Takes care. Great care and effort," Ernestine said while wrestling the tarp. "I'll lose 'em all if I don't get them covered. Do you feel that?"

"The chill?"

"Yes, the chill. The blasted chill. Showed up this morning. My eldest is scheduled to visit this Saturday and I planned to ask him to do this then, but if I wait that long, they'll be ruined. Just ruined. Frost will kill my babies." A bright pink flush enveloped Ernestine's face and the sliver of neck peeking out from her high collar.

Rosarie grabbed the tarp, one corner in each delicate hand. "Ernestine, dear, you're soaked to the bone. The wind is whipping the bayou right at us today."

Ernestine ignored her, shaking the tarp free of mist while she stretched it the length of four fat bushes.

"You're gonna catch your death out here. We both will." Rosarie jerked on her end of the tarp—a poor imitation of Ernestine's actions.

"Not if we work fast," Ernestine said and spit a long, grey tendril from the corner of her mouth. Her hair flew this way and that. Halfway through pinning her long braid into a bun that morning, she felt the chill and ran for the tarps. "Now, hold tight to those corners and toss the tarp in the air like a sheet. The wind should allow it to land softly. Don't yank it down. Let the wind work for you." Ernestine glanced at Rosarie, bit down on her bottom lip, then thrust the tarp in the air. Bayou spray slapped both of the women in the face, but the center billowed up like a balloon and floated down soft as honey. "Now tie each corner to the bottom of a fat stem. And careful of the thorns. They're good and sharp."

Good and sharp indeed. After an hour of tossing and tying and fighting the wind, Rosarie had two rips in her right sleeve, all the way through the woolen plaid bodice and her heavy silk blouse.

"Your arm is bleeding," Ernestine said, wiping her forehead with a handkerchief.

Rosarie glanced at her arm. "Just a scratch. One of the thorns got me good I guess."

"Well, let's get inside. Get that taken care of."

"No, no. It's nothing. I should be getting home."

"Nonsense. I know for a fact you've got hours before that husband of yours will be home. It being Thursday and all." Ernestine smacked her hands together, knocking off bits of black soil, and climbed her front porch stairs. Frowning, Rosarie followed the old woman up the stairs and into her house.

Ernestine had long ago become numb to the musty smell of her home. Dust lay undisturbed on every surface. Stacks of unread novels leaned against tattered, upholstered wing-backed chairs. A bin near the parlor fireplace overflowed with discarded newspaper, intended for kindling but forgotten. Rosarie stifled a cough as she maneuvered around the first of several side tables.

"How long has it been since we had tea in your kitchen? Must be before Walter's stroke, if I'm remembering correctly." Rosarie nearly knocked the black physician's bag resting on one of the side tables to the floor. She secured the bag and wiped the dust from her hands on her soil-stained overskirt. "Were summer and fall as busy for you as for me?"

"I imagine so. Come on to the kitchen. I've got a bandage back here. Oh, and tea, of course. Let's have some tea. Thursday afternoons are the perfect day for tea, don't you agree?"

Rosarie flinched. "You don't have to do that. Tea that is. And the bandage. I'm fine, really. The bleeding has practically ceased."

"Nonsense. Come. Sit." Ernestine pointed to a wooden chair, southern pine with leaf carvings at the rounded corners.

Unlike the parlor and dining room and the entire second floor the kitchen was meticulous. Not a single crumb or speck of dirt lay on the floor. The small table with carvings that matched the chairs was rubbed to a high shine. When Ernestine opened both doors of an equally polished sideboard, Rosarie saw shelves full of small vials and bottles; each labeled and set in shallow, straight rows. Ernestine grabbed a square metal box labeled *gauze bandages* and set it on the table next to Rosarie.

"Go on and roll up that sleeve so I can see what I'm working with." Ernestine turned from Rosarie. With a long, iron hook and two steady hands she moved the kettle from the fire to the table. She placed two china saucers and cups abloom with tiny, pink roses near the kettle and frowned as she turned one saucer, hoping Rosarie wouldn't notice the chip. After Rosarie poured the tea, Ernestine dragged a chair close to her and sat, expelling a sigh on her way down. "You're gonna need to roll up the blouse sleeve too, although we might as well cut it off. That's quite a tear. Those thorns can do some damage, can't they."

"Oh, I can mend that. No need to ruin a perfectly good blouse. Who knows when I will be able to replace it."

"Well, the person who would know that is you. Don't you help Mister Hodges with the ordering? Just order yourself a new blouse."

"I really shouldn't. My armoire is a bit full already. I can mend it." Rosarie unbuttoned the starched cuff of her ripped, blood-stained blouse. "And Mister Hodges prefers to do the ordering himself. I just help out in the mornings at the counter while he checks the stock. 'Inventory must be done daily,' he says."

"Well, at least you get to help him a little," Ernestine said as she rose and crossed to the basin. "My Walter never let me lift a finger as far as his practice went. He always said that he'll provide outside the home and I'll provide inside." Ernestine flashed a wicked grin as she wrung out a clean, white cloth over the basin. "But I did pick up a few things from him over the years. Such as how to clean a wound. 'Cleanliness is next to Godliness and God will help you heal,' he says." Ernestine stopped short when she reached the table and glanced at Rosarie's arm. "My roses didn't do that." She stared at the deep purple and green bruise that encased Rosarie's forearm. "What on Earth?"

"Oh, that. It's nothing. Just a bruise. I bruise so easily, and they just take forever to heal. I guess God's not helping me much with that. He probably has too much on his plate already to worry with my bruising. It should clear up in a few days, and hopefully, I won't do that—"

"Rosarie Hodges, I raised three boys who only talked like that when they were trying to hide what really happened. Now, how did you hurt your arm? How long has it been like this?" Ernestine touched the bruise with two gentle fingers, feeling a bit of heat. Then, she rotated Rosarie's arm. The underside, which should have been fish-belly white, was a rainbow of noxious colors. "It looks like someone grabbed—"

Ernestine set Rosarie's arm back on the table and turned to the gauze box and damp rag. "Let's get those scratches cleaned and covered."

For several minutes, the women sat in silence as Ernestine cleaned the wound with the damp cloth.

"Ernestine," Rosarie said, quiet and unsteady. "I would appreciate you not...well, you know how people gossip in this town. Rumors can cause trouble."

Ernestine opened the polished sideboard again, retrieving a small bottle labeled *antiseptic*. "Now, this is going to sting a bit, but it will help the wound stay clean." She splashed a few drops on Rosarie's arm. "Hold still. Just a few drops more." Then, Ernestine blew on the cuts as a mother blows on a toddler's knee.

"What is that? It feels like a thousand bee stings." Rosarie continued blowing on her arm after Ernestine stood up to grab a gauze strip.

"It's called *antiseptic*. According to my Walter, a man named Lister found that this stuff helps keeps cuts clean so they won't fester." Ernestine began wrapping the gauze around Rosarie's forearm careful not to touch the cuts or surrounding bruises.

"It must do something because it's still stinging."

"Just give it a minute or two. The stings will stop." Ernestine locked eyes with Rosarie then looked back at the bottle of antiseptic on the table. "Several years back, Walter and I went to Philadelphia for a medical convention. Well, Walter went for the convention. I went for the gardens. So many! Tulips and lilies and hyacinth and hydrangeas. Terribly difficult buggers to grow, hydrangeas. Of course, my favorite were the roses. Every color you could imagine.

Ernestine folded the remaining gauze into a small, neat rectangle and returned it to the metal bin. "I begged Walter to let me bring home clippings to add to the garden, but he said there wasn't room in the baggage car for souvenirs. Of course, there was plenty of room for all his bottles and whatnots. He must have brought home twenty bottles of this stuff. This is the last one."

Ernestine tightened the cap on the bottle of antiseptic. "Keep the bandage clean through the night. Tomorrow morning, take it off and let the cut air out a bit. I found with my boys that a bit of airing out always helped. Walter told me that was a bunch of hokey, but I told him mothers did his job long before he came along."

"How is he doing? Any improvement?" Rosarie glanced at the open space in the doorway just in front of her.

"He's sleeping right now. Had a terrible, fretful night last night. Neither of us got much sleep." Ernestine placed the bottle and metal box of gauze back in the sideboard, then folded the rag and placed it next to the basin.

"I can wash that for you and return it to you in a couple of days," Rosarie offered.

"No need. The laundry girl comes tomorrow."

A grandfather clock chimed from the hallway causing Walter to snort and Ernestine to flinch. "That's my Walter. Every time that clock chimes he snorts. Hated it before all this happened."

"Seems he still can make his opinions known," Rosarie said with a smile.

"Yes. Yes, he can and does. But you best get on home. Mister Hodges will be expecting supper in a few hours. Or does he eat elsewhere on Thursdays?"

Rosarie stood, careful not to bump her arm against the table or chair. "Thank you for the bandage and the tea. I need to get supper going."

"Of course."

Rosarie paused before the leaning tower of books. "He doesn't go there anymore."

"Go where, dear? Who?"

"Since Ruth White died. Mister Hodges no longer goes there on Thursday afternoons. You needn't meddle so."

"By the looks of your arm, somebody needs to meddle. For your sake."

"Mister Hodges has troubles. Ones that I cannot help him with, so I do what I can."

"My Walter had plenty of troubles, but he never laid a hand on me. Not once."

Rosarie stepped toward Ernestine and gestured to the clutter and then toward Walter's bedroom. "We all have our troubles."

***

For the next week, Ernestine did what she did every day—tended her roses. But, that week, she found herself examining her roses from the street side. Every so often she glanced at Rosarie's porch. Rosarie didn't leave her house often that week, claiming her typical stomach pain was worse than usual. The pain did not prevent her, Ernestine noted, from pushing a chair closer to her front parlor window so that she could peer through the drapes. All was well with hiding and roses and gardening and denials until Sunday rolled around. Sunday mornings did not allow for hibernation or chores. Sunday mornings in Huet Pointe were to be spent Mass at Our Lady of Sorrow. Attendance was mandatory.

Rosarie had pinned her veil low enough on her head to hide her husband's latest Thursday cruelty, but as she descended the steps after Mass, the wind kicked up the front corner of lace. On the front lawn, Ernestine chatted up Father Healy. As they discussed altar décor for the Christmas masses, Ernestine glimpsed a bit of purple near Rosarie's temple.

Later, Ernestine knocked on Rosarie's front door. "Rosarie, I know you're home. I can smell the lamb."

Rosarie scurried past Mr. Hodges, engrossed at the dining table studying out-of-date financial reports. She opened the door and slipped through it, the only sound being the swish-swish of her skirts. Outside with the door closed behind her, she spoke. "Ernestine, how lovely to see you. What can I do for you?"

"Well, first you can stop acting so sweet. I know my standing here's sending shivers up your spine."

"No, no, no. Really, I'm happy to see you."

"Is that why you've been hiding in your house all week, peeking through those blinds?"

"What? No. I've been a bit under the weather. Probably from helping you with your roses."

"What you're doing is trying to hide another bruise. And you did a fine job until the wind got you on those steps."

"Hush." Rosarie motioned to Ernestine to lower her voice. "Mister Hodges is right inside. If you care for me at all you will keep your voice down. Or better yet, don't worry about my bruises. They are my business to deal with."

"I don't think you're dealing with them at all. What are you doing to make him stop?"

Rosarie stood as frozen as the shallow puddle in her birdbath.

"Nothing. You've done nothing to make him stop. And you'll continue to do nothing until he kills you. Then *nothing* can be done except plant roses on your grave."

Rosarie had no reply but to purse her lips together.

"That's what I thought." Ernestine turned. As she lumbered down the stairs, she said, loud enough for only Rosarie and the angels to hear, "Come see me when you've had enough."

***

Enough didn't come fast enough for Ernestine. On Christmas Eve, after she'd finished cooking and wrapped the last of the Christmas candy for her grandchildren and, of course, Father Healy, she fashioned one more gift: A basket of cherry cordials, two yards of white linen, one bottle of a fine white powder, and a note.

Dearest Rosarie, Ernestine had written in rickety, labored penmanship.

May the New Year bring you peace and comfort. If it doesn't, sprinkle this powder in Mr. Hodges trousers. He will find himself too busy scratching to use his hands for anything else.

Merry Christmas,
Ernestine Harris

P.S. The linen is for a new blouse.

Lulu

To IGNORE THE SWAMP IS A FOOL'S GAME. It takes on many forms—ponds, creeks, rivers, even a trickle of a stream over smooth rocks. It may swell to a lake in places, with roped cedars rising in shadows, sometimes five, six feet wide. A pirogue can snake through the tall reeds then float onto the deafening quiet of a lagoon. There, the cedars disappear. The expanse of water suggests safe passage, but consider what lies beneath the murky surface. Cedar stumps, those mighty trees Mother Nature with her impulsive temperament deemed cut down for whatever reason, hold their ground. Wait to be known. Only a fool forgets the stumps or underestimates their treacherous value.

"If I was born with a last name, no one bothered to tell me." Lulu grabbed the whiskey bottle and poured two fingers into a cut crystal glass. She slid the bottle back across the table. "Help yourself, Father."

"Thank you." The priest glanced the empty glass before pouring. "This is lovely. New Orleans?"

"New York. A present to myself. Surely you have a set over in the rectory."

"Not this nice."

"Well, temptations of the flesh." Lulu tipped her glass toward the priest.

He eyed her, but not with contempt. His slate blue eyes suggested an understanding. "You should come to the church. I imagine confession is a necessity in your line of work."

"Needing and doing are two very different things. And, to confess, shouldn't I be truly sorry, at least attempt repentance?"

"Ideally, yes." Father Healy flinched against a clash of thunder, one so invasive the oil lamps flickered. A drop of scotch splashed against the table.

"Little jumpy tonight, Father? Not quite used to the rumblings of Huet Pointe? Well, then, why don't you just sit in that comfy chair, drink my good scotch from my lovely glass, and enjoy the view." Lulu waved her right hand toward the open parlor, draped in purple velvet with settees, sofas, and chairs draped in women too old to be brides and too young to be wives. That scrumptious age when half-dressed can be accomplished without guilt or regret or shame. Shame had no place in the House of Dann. "That is why you come to see me, correct? Even on those nights you must fight the wet and cold? Or are you one of those types who believe God will prevent you from succumbing to the demon flu?" Lulu still carried herself with the ego of that lesser age, but by the time Father Healy began his weekly visits, she had earned petticoats, overskirts, full corset, and sleeves, the privileges of a madam.

"God's protection is nothing to scoff at." Father Healy dabbed his finger against the errant drop then licked his fingertip clean. "I like to care for all my flock, not just those who fulfill their weekly obligation." He looked about the room, unrevealing of whether he admired the décor or the product.

"Because my name is written in your Book of Lambs? I think you'll find a hundred Lulabells and Lurlines and even a few Lulus, but none of them me. I wasn't born into your registry."

"But one may be you."

"Of course not, Padre. God has no idea what my name is. I made it up, the last part. Some things can only be accomplished with a full name. As you can see, I had goals. Things to accomplish with that free will you harp about. See, Rev, back then, when I's lying beneath some sweaty mass of a man, I'd imagine myself

with his last name. Lulu Jones. Lulu Thompson. Lulu Little. Not
Little. A lifetime with that turd would've been a slow death by
constant, boring twaddle and barely noticeable *twaddling*." Lulu
laughed, something she did when she thought of her beginnings
and was sober enough to laugh. "Lulu Boudreaux? Hell, with all
the Boudreauxs in these parts that coulda been my real last name."

Father Healy downed his scotch, licked his lips for any stray
drops, and reached for the bottle as if waiting to have his hand
slapped away. He was a naughty child who wanted too many
cookies.

"So, on one particular night," Lulu continued, "the man pumping and thrusting on top of me like he's trying to turn sweat into
butter was a Love. No, not my *love*. I wanted a last name, but not
his. Every time he came to see me, I'd crack up at the irony. Mister
Love and his whore."

"Is that how you think of yourself? The whore?" Healy lifted
his full glass to his nose and inhaled.

"You know, that stuff works a whole lot better if you drink
it. Anyway, that's what I am, well, was. I've no shame in how I
started." Lulu pounded her own glass empty, her jade eyes barely
closing against the singe on the back of her throat. "Mister Love
was sweet, but that man played my nerves better than he coulda
ever played my ... well you know." A grin flashed across Lulu's face
at the sight of the blush heating up Healy's. "Or maybe you don't?
Surely you had yourself a taste before tuckin' it away for good."

Healy met Lulu's eyes and held her stare for a moment as
if allowing her to enjoy teasing him. "I believe you were in the
middle of a story," he said then took another sip while the storm
outside threatened to burst through the doors.

"Sure. Sure. So, Mister Love insisted I talk to him all the while.
Not dirty, filthy words like you men like. Well, maybe not you."
She curled one corner of her mouth and waited for a reaction that
didn't come. "Anyway, he wanted me to talk to him like I actually,

truthfully loved him. Poor thing. He had no idea I'm incapable of such a feeling."

"Everyone is born with the capacity to love."

"I don't doubt that. But I believe that capacity can be drained. Like the swamp at low tide. Or that muddy street out there. Eventually all that water will just disappear."

"So, you believe that your capacity to love—that great gift of God—has been drained from you? Just disappeared?"

"Father, I told you already. This isn't confession. I've just no need for love. Love's got no place in my life. I mean who in this world has shown me love? My momma? I assume she's the one who brought me to Ruth in the first place. My daddy? I'm guessing if he knew about me and gave a damn, I'd have had a last name and wouldn't have spent eight years as 'Second story, two doors down the hall Lulu.' Eight damn years under that woman's thumb and any man she sent to my room."

Father Healy reached for a third pass on the bottle, but Lulu grabbed it instead. "How 'bout something of substance in that belly of yours? Chip," she called to the barkeep, "Get Father here a big steak. You like it a little bloody?"

"I like it any way you wanna fix it."

"Well, Chip'll fry it up for you. I don't cook for anybody but myself." Lulu poured scotch in her own glass, watching as the brown liquid raised three fingers high. "Now, Mister Love. Lord, he was a strange breed of sinner. That night Mister Love went on and on with his usual 'Lulu, my pet, my sweet,' and then waiting for me to respond. 'Oh, yes, my love, yes,' I'd tell him. I may not know love, but I'm a damn fine actress. I shoulda been on a stage in front of thousands for the talent it took to utter those words to Mister Huey Love. Mister Huey Love of Huet Pointe. Silly name for a silly man."

The priest allowed a short chortle to escape his lips.

"Careful, Father, the scotch is showing." Lulu smiled, almost. It was the kind of smile that betrayed the thick armor she had crafted link by link so that seeing beneath it was as difficult as through muddy water. "That dullard Love kept it going like that the whole time. 'What else, my pet? How do I love you?' Then, he'd prop himself up on his elbows so his face was directly above mine. So close I smelled his dinner. He wanted me to express to him for the thousandth time that what he was doing to me was exactly what I needed. That his churning was the best I'd known. Well, I was all out of biscuits, so I didn't need no butter."

To that, Father Healy choked a bit, allowing a dribble of scotch to fall from his mouth to his chin.

"Chip needs to hurry with that steak. I don't need a sloppy man in here tonight." Lulu offered Father Healy a linen napkin.

"My apologies," said Father Healy, blotting his chin.

"Now, where was I before Mister Love and his silly pounding invaded my thoughts? Oh, yes, I remember. Incapable of love. Father, what purpose could love serve? Even if I'd tried. Cleaned myself up. Moved to New Orleans to start a new beginning and trapped myself a husband. To what end? Become his whore? Love didn't get the job done. Love didn't improve my station. Love didn't give me security or take care of old Ruth. Hell, Mister Love wouldn't even get off my hair that night with those damn elbows a' his before several strands ripped out of my head! 'Sweetheart, my hair. It's pulling,' I told him. 'Oh, goodness. Have I hurt you? I never wish to hurt you, my love. May I kiss the pain away?' he asked. I wanted to tell him, 'Just move your fat elbow,' but I didn't." Lulu drained her glass and poured another three fingers. "Insulting a man never gets ya a good tip."

"Perhaps Chip should fry a steak for you as well."

Lulu ignored the priest, as if he hadn't spoken at all. "Instead, I'd say, 'Certainly. I can think of nothing better' or some kind of nonsense like that. Then he'd press his lips against my forehead allowing beads a' sweat to drip onto my face. If Ruth had allowed me more than one bath per week, she might have—" Lulu pressed her lips closed and breathed deeply through her nose. "Low tide. I bet the stumps are showing. The rain's churning up all that bottom stink. You know under the sandy layer; the bottom is just black clay. Full of sulfur. Stinks so bad you can taste it."

"Yes, the air here can be a bit foul."

"One of God's jokes, huh? Huet Pointe? Not that I'll ever leave this place, but I can't imagine a place more green, water more beautiful with all its colors. But underneath is all rotten eggs and gator shit." Lulu tugged the front right side of her corset, feeling her body swell from the scotch. "Ruth thought the basin and pitcher were enough to remove every stench around here ... the sulfur bubbling up from the mud, the incense she burned every night, Mister Love's stench, that foul concoction of body hair, whiskey, meat, and smoke. And that musty cologne he'd doused himself in that never fooled anybody."

Chip appeared and placed a piping hot T-bone on the table, along with a matching knife and fork made of pure silver.

"Chip, dear, I'd like one of those. And a roll, if there are any left from dinner service." As Chip smiled and padded away, gratefulness swelled in Lulu's chest, just as bothersome as the scotch-sweat. She swallowed hard against it. "Back to the story at hand and Mister Love. 'Oh, my love, my love,' I'd say, just to throw him a bone now and then." Lulu sipped her drink, a chaser to end her tangent and focus her mind. "See, if I played it up a bit, he'd sneak a few coins to me before paying Ruth. Mister Love was always good for a nice tip."

"So this Ruth," Father Healy said, "she was before my time here. Was she—"

"Oh, yes. Miss Ruth White. There's a name for you. Biblical and clean. I doubt that woman ever spent a minute of her life with a Bible in her hand, 'cept maybe to spank somebody with it. Anyway, originally this place was called Mary's, but it became Ruth's when Ruth poisoned Mary one night. That's the confession you should have taken. Everybody thinks that old Mother Mary's death was a tragic accident, but I know different. Ruth's truth was part of my introduction to the life on my thirteenth birthday. The cleaver she'd kill me with if I spilt the beans was part two. You know she called that damn thing The Keeper? Crazy ol' bat."

Lulu refreshed her glass. She took a sip, swished it around her mouth, and gulped it down with no flinch or wince at all.

"My thoughts have run amuck again. What was it I wanted to tell you? Oh, yes, the story. Before any payment from that night, I had two hundred and twelve dollars and thirty-five cents hidden in the toe of my spare boots. Not bad for one year of saving. I figured if I saved thirty dollars a month, I'd have enough for train fare west with plenty left over to purchase property in six months' time. I figured there weren't many white working girls out there. All Mex or Injun. I bet white women fetch pretty high tips. That was my plan. I'd work, same as always, for a couple years until I didn't have to work at all. Then I'd buy a place and collect a Ruth's share for myself. But I'd treat my girls real good. And I do. My girls bathe least twice a week. Clean and happy. 'Specially if they're real sweet and playful like I was. I always ended things with Mister Love with a 'Are you quite satisfied, my love?' And I did that night, too. I even smiled at him after having to watch his big, nekkid rear-end jiggle across the room. Big, pale glob of shiny fluff, something that should be rolled into a pastry, not striding across my bedroom."

Father Healy allowed a chewed bite of the tender filet to slide down his throat. "Perhaps I should check on your steak."

"If I smiled and made goo-goo eyes at Love, he'd pull a few bucks out of his breeches for me, 'fore he paid Ruth. Then he'd pull on the rest and head downstairs to settle up with Ruth."

The priest poured himself another glass but stopped at two fingers rather than Lulu's three.

"Now, on that night, as I did every time, I tucked the bills inside my spare boot and threw on my robe, a silk kimono given to me by another of my regulars. If I dawdled in my room too long after Love left, Ruth grabbed the strap, *Ruth's Reminder* she called it. I can't remember how many times she came after my legs like I was a damn child."

Chip placed a steak in front of her, cut neatly away from the bone. A roll with two pats of butter sat next to it soaking up the red juices.

"Thank you, dear," she muttered and took a bite of the roll. While chewing, she continued. "So, I come out of my room, heading for the parlor, but damn if I only made it to the second story landing 'fore I saw him. A daggum Lawry standing there talking to Ruth. Now, you not being from Huet Pointe, you don't know the whole of the Lawry gang. These boys were mean and dirty, made Mister Love smell as sweet as strawberries. I ducked my butt back in the hallway and pinned myself against the wall. Dammit if I wasn't gonna stick there until he left or got sent to another girl. 'You want who, Mister Lawry?' Ruth asked him. 'The blonde one. Lulu.' I could practically hear the spit spraying from his nasty mouth. 'She just finished up,' Ruth told him. Then, 'Give her a minute.' Then he said it. The words no girl wanted to hear. 'I think you misunderstood me. I want her. I mean we want her for our own. I got fifty bucks right here for her.'" Lulu paused for a bite of steak.

"The steak is delicious. So tender it barely needs to be chewed."

"So, Ruth goes, 'You want me to sell Lulu to you?' 'Yes'em,' that bastard answered. *Yes'em.* Like he was buying cattle. Well, by now I was in a panic, could feel my heart poundin'. But that bitch Ruth ain't never passed up money. 'Thought you boys had Sabine. She not to your liking anymore?' she asked. And he said, 'Sabine's

Daddy's girl. He's made it clear that none of us touch her.' Ruth, always ready to haggle with you men, she says, 'So, you thought you'd strut in here and buy my best girl? Fifty ain't enough, Mister Lawry."

Another pour and another gulp of scotch warmed Lulu's throat. She slammed the empty glass on the table.

"That woman was hagglin' with my life. And she knew what they'd do to me if they owned me. But she didn't care. All she ever cared about was her fat pockets. So fat she had to fill the floorboards with it. 'I'll take no less than a hundred. Come back in the morning. I'll get her cleaned up nice and fresh for you.' As soon as that front door swung shut, I knew what I had to do. My robe was whippin' in the wind, I got back to my room so fast. I flung open my trunk and dumped everything on the floor. I don't know why I's hoping that two hundred and twelve dollars and thirty-five cents had multiplied into something more, but it hadn't and it wasn't enough. I knew soon as the sun was up, those Lawry boys be back lookin' to take me home for their first not-rented-by-the-hour taste. Uh uh. No. I know Sabine. I seen that look in her eyes. Ain't no man gonna cause me to have that look."

The priest chewed his last bite of steak, grinding the meat with wide eyes fixed on Lulu.

"But with buying a horse, 'specially at that late hour, then a coach from New Orleans to as far west as I could afford, not to mention buying luggage and a dress or two so I didn't look like I was runnin', well you can see why that paper and coin wasn't gonna last long. So, I made the only decision I could. I decided to steal what I needed from Ruth."

"I see, I see," Father Healy said, then asked, "So this is confession?"

Lulu glared at him. "I told you I'm not sorry for a damn thing so there's nothing to confess." Lulu tugged at the ruffle atop her corset. "So, like I said, I didn't have a choice. And, if you really think about it, I was only gonna steal my portion. You can't steal what should belong to you in the first place. It-a been years since she laid on her back for anyone other than her own choosing. So, I got myself dressed and headed downstairs. Ruth was nowhere to be seen. I figured her Mister Hodges—he always visited Ruth on Thursdays—I figured those two were making it in her bedroom. So, I snuck in the pantry. It wasn't no sooner that I'd pried that loose board up and had two hundred in my hand that that pantry door flew open. Ruth and Mister Hodges starin' at me through the doorway. 'I come for a bottle,' Ruth said, 'but it looks like we found us a rat instead.'"

"What'd you do?" Father Healy pushed his plate to the side, placing his linen napkin on top of his discarded bone and silverware.

"Started beggin' like a ninny. That's probably the worst part of all of this, how I begged that woman to forget all about it. Begged her not to sell me to the Lawrys. Begged her to forgive me for trying to steal that money. That part leaves a real sour taste. But she didn't care. She dragged me into the kitchen, handed The Keeper all shiny and sharpened to Mister Hodges then held my arm flat against the cutting board. If it weren't for one thought she'da chopped off my hand."

"What thought was that?" A fresh squall churned outside as sideways rain pounded the windows.

"That a one-handed whore won't fetch much money. That's what made Ruth only take a finger." Lulu held up her left hand, revealing the nub where a pointer finger should have been. "She told me I should kiss her feet for not taking fingers off the right. 'You can still give a handy, nice and proper,' she said. After that all I remember is the lamplight bouncing off The Keeper as it came down. And waking up two days later."

"Seems a bit harsh since I assume you didn't keep the money."

"Not hers or mine. Not a dime. Woke up with nothin' but a dress hanging on the door and a bloody, throbbing hand. It took me three years to earn my saved money back. She said she couldn't get as much for me no more, what with being damaged and all. Like the decision to use The Keeper was mine."

"You poor child."

"No need for that, Padre. Cause of Ruth and her cruelty I finally found my name."

"Dann?" Father Healy asked. "Did you find your family?"

"Of course not. If I had family, if I knew them, no way I'd stay on here. Do this. Or they'd make me just to get their cut, like they deserve one. No, I told you. I made up my name. Dann. Dann with two Ns."

"The fifth son of Jacob?"

"That's the one. See, I read the Bible. Especially when I's laid in bed ate up with fever from what that bitch Ruth did. That's when I found him. Dann. Judge. Provider of justice. Son of Jacob and his concubine. Son of a whore." Lulu grinned then a sadness flashed across her face.

"Yes, but he did not beget one of the twelve tribes. He was – "

"As far as you know. So the Bible doesn't list him in your precious registry either. Just like me. No one paid attention. No one cared what she did to me. Ruth never did. She never cared to read no Bible. Learn about her name. Somebody gave her a name and she just took it and had no idea what it meant. Never cared to learn a damn thing other than how to be cruel and selfish. Do you know that Ruth means friend and beauty?"

Father Healy nodded, fingering his empty glass on the table.

"But how does a name like that chop off somebody's finger and not feel a bit of remorse? And I know I should forgive her, let it alone. Forgiveness, right? Ask Almighty God for the ability to forgive. After all, things worked out pretty nice for me here." A satisfied grin flashed across Lulu's face. "She's some of that gator shit now, you know. Old Tarasque got her. Chewed her up and swallered her down. Most of her anyway."

"Yes, I've heard the rumors. Apparently not the beast's first victim."

"No. I'm pretty sure he's been feeding on us as long as we been here."

Father Healy stifled a burp or maybe a gag. Lulu wasn't sure and didn't care.

"Lulu, please, I beg you, for your sake. Make a confession." Father Healy's glance was tender, almost tender enough. "Ask forgiveness."

Lulu popped the last bit of bloody steak between her teeth and chewed, licking the corner of her mouth before speaking. "For what? I've done nothing wrong. Like I said before, confession's for the sorry." Lulu emptied her glass one last time and stood, leaning against the table for support. She motioned to a pretty brunette lounging on the settee. The girl, too old to be a bride, too young to be a wife, but just the right age for the House of Dann, sauntered to Lulu's side. Lulu laced one slender arm through her employee's arm and leaned a bit into her shoulder. "See ya next Tuesday, Padre." The two turned from the table, leaving Healy alone with dirty plates and empty glasses. Lulu's stiff taffeta rubbed against the girl's chiffon and lace all the way up the stairs.

Part Four: Spring

Bonnie

"It must appear that a man could encircle my waist with his hands. That's what Mother says." Bonnie McLeary held tight to the bedpost as the corset compressed her ribs. "My ability to breathe properly is of little importance." She swallowed a cough as Tilly, her mother's maid, tugged on the laces.

With her right leg hiked up and foot planted in the small of Bonnie's back, Tilly grunted. Her dark, coiled hair was soaked with sweat, so much so that the tignon wrapped around her head, intended to hide her offensive locks from the too-delicate Huet Pointe high society, fast became an ineffective dam. Beads of sweat broke free and rolled into her dark chocolate eyes. When she swiped at the naughty droplets, her left leg gave way. Her grip on the corset laces, however, remained firm as she tumbled backwards to the floor.

"Oh!" Bonnie yelped, landing squarely on Tilly, now buried under several petticoats. "What in Creation is wrong with you, Tilly?" Bonnie grasped the embroidered quilt on the bed and pulled herself upright. "Get up and try again. I can still move a bit, so I know it's not tight enough."

Tilly nodded and stood, soaking her sleeve as she wiped it across her forehead.

Bonnie patted her blonde ringlets, meticulously placed to frame her cherub face. "You didn't muss my hair, did you?"

Tilly shook her head, only glancing at Bonnie long enough to confirm the low chignon and strategically placed ringlets were still intact.

"Good." Bonnie turned and assumed her position again at the bedpost. "Now try not to fall again. I know we can get this right. Everything must be perfect. You've no idea what tonight could lead to. Or, as Mother says, how disastrous my circumstances will be if all does not go well." Disastrous indeed, for Bonnie had her heart set on only one outcome.

Tilly nodded and grabbed the corset laces. She wrapped one lace around each small hand and bit on her bottom lip, ready to test the boning and stitching of the corset.

"Mother says once I am dressed, I am to wait here for my cue to enter the party. Father was going to escort me down the stai... Oh! That was a good one, Tilly. One more hard tug should do it." Bonnie stretched her fingers along her waist, measuring each side. "Well, maybe two more." She craned her neck to look at Tilly. "I cannot believe he went and shot himself in the face before my debut. How careless. He should have put aside his morning hunts until after he and mother secured my engagement. Muskets are such stupid contraptions. All the jamming and misfiring and what-not. He should have known to be more careful. Doing this to me. And to Mama! Why would he... And now I've gone and gotten myself upset." Bonnie sucked in all the air her corset allowed and blew out slowly with intention through two perfectly plump, pink lips. "No more of that, Tilly. If I start prattling on about Daddy again, you are to yank those laces so hard you flip me backward. Again. Understand?" She craned her neck to glance at Tilly a second time.

Again, Tilly nodded her obedience and gave the laces two more strong jerks then tied the laces in a double bow to prevent any give.

Bonnie had heard the shot that threw her father from his horse the previous fall but thought nothing of it as she performed her morning dressing ritual. She had no clue that the blow was so direct both her father's feet kicked out of his stirrups. "A small blessing," Bonnie later heard the staff proclaim, for who knows where the startled horse might have dragged Gil McLeary's body otherwise.

It wasn't until the commotion began—screams and cries from a few female field hands—that Bonnie knew anything was the matter. When she peered out her window, past the first fallen leaves of the season, she recognized the golden-brown boots lying on the ground. A second blessing, unknown to her, was that her father's mangled face was turned toward the creek rather than her window and the palatial white house she called home.

Bonnie remembered backing away from her window. She remembered throwing on her dressing gown before leaving her bedroom and running down the stairs. Her bare feet dashed across the sprawling, wrap-around porch and past the hedge of Angel's Trumpets. She remembered her mother's arms and her mother's words, "This changes nothing." Bonnie couldn't remember if her mother's face was streaked with tears or not.

"As Mother says, today is a day of celebration, the celebration of my life to be, not—" Bonnie stopped herself. "Enough. Right, Tilly? Okay. Now for the overskirt. Can you get it by yourself or will you need assistance? I cannot believe Mother assigned only you to help me. Surely she could've spared one more."

Tilly, with great care not to crimp the massive circle of white silk, teetered on a footstool as she draped one half of the skirt over each of her arms. She flipped the rear of the skirt over her head, revealing perfect French seams down the eight panels that created the bell. Now blinded by the silk, Tilly grasped the waistline and bent forward, arms and silk outstretched, muscles twitching from the weight.

"Okay. Now hold still. If this skirt touches my hair, we'll have to start over." Bonnie, like a diver slipping into slick water, threaded herself through the waistline. "Okay, now flip it over me. Careful. Careful."

With some force, Tilly flipped the back of the skirt over Bonnie and watched as an ivory sea billowed and found its resting place atop Bonnie's petticoats. A smile spread across Tilly's face. Bonnie's hair was perfect, not a single curl out of place.

"Perfect," Bonnie said. "And you didn't fall off the stool this time. I knew our rehearsals were worth the time. Now for the top."

Tilly lifted the bodice off the bed and held it open as Bonnie slipped her lithe arms through the boned and embellished bodice. Tilly then scurried behind Bonnie to fasten the seventeen tiny pearl buttons down Bonnie's back. Bonnie's mother had ordered one pearl for each year of her daughter's life.

As Tilly worked the buttons, Bonnie smoothed the skirt beneath the bodice edge. "I think the final design is perfect, don't you? And firing the first seamstress may have been a bit cruel, but necessary. Her own fault, really. If she'd taken the time to listen to Mother and me regarding what we wanted, she may have been able to salvage that fiasco she created. A scoop neckline? Really? So passé. Was I to present myself to my future husband in last year's fashion? What would that have said? That I haven't the means to keep up, that's what. Or worse, that I would be satisfied with less than perfect. You can't build a marriage on low expectations. That's what Mother says. And Mother and Daddy were married for how long? Two decades before he—"

Tilly yanked the nape of the Bonnie's bodice, forcing her to step backward.

"What was? Oh, thank you. I almost started in on Daddy again, didn't I? You actually do understand what I ask of you, don't you, Tilly? Your tongue may be useless, but your ears are right as rain." Bonnie turned toward the maid. "All done? Well, what do you think?"

Tilly stepped back and gazed at Bonnie. The maid moved her eyes slowly from toes to nose for dramatic affect. She smiled at the young woman and, with two hands, blew Bonnie a kiss of approval.

"Thank you," Bonnie said, walking to the gilded mirror on the far wall. As she stood in the mirror admiring the line of her bare shoulders against the beaded neckline, her mother, still in the traditional mourning color of black, peeked into Bonnie's bedroom.

"Tilly, are you –" She pushed the door wide as she caught her first glimpse of the finished product: Her daughter, exquisite as a field of Edelweiss, before the mirror. "Bonnie, you are splendid!" She crossed to her daughter and adjusted the bow placed one inch below Bonnie's right shoulder. "I was a bit worried that these bows were fussy or childish, but I think you were right on insisting we add them. They add just the right amount of playfulness you'll find men want in a wife. Heaven knows your father enjoyed playing."

In the weeks following Gil McLeary's funeral and burial, Bonnie had begun to question her parents' love for each other. It wasn't just her mother's odd first words to Bonnie as her father lay dead in the pasture—*This changes nothing*. It was her insistence that the debut still happen as scheduled. Her refusal to postpone. Her mother's insistence that her father's funeral be without fanfare, over and done with as if it were a menial chore to complete before returning to debut preparations. She'd never given the subject of her parents' union a second's thought before that terrible morning, before Bonnie herself faced the prospect of a loveless marriage.

"Mother, I wish you didn't have to wear black this evening. Do you even mourn Daddy?"

"That's not the point. Custom is custom and must be followed. The slightest insult to any of the matrons downstairs will ruin you, Bonnie. That is a chance I am not willing to take. Although you are now without a father, you are still well bred, educated, graceful, everything they should want in a daughter. You are still more than what they should want for their sons."

"But the emerald green on you was so rich. Won't the black just remind everyone of our current predicament? And if you are no longer mourning in your heart—"

"You think I'm no longer in mourning?" Anna Beth's words bit at Bonnie, as if pronouncing them burnt the tongue. "I miss your father every day."

"Do you?"

"Of course. Now shush. Everyone knows of our recent loss and how that unfortunate event might lower your station. They will try to use that as a mark against you. That's why you, my darling, must be aware of everything you do tonight."

"Yes." Bonnie stared at her reflection as she recited her mother's instructions. "Keep the conversation on weather and art and travel. Keep my laughter light and my voice pleasant. Small sips of champagne only."

"Correct. You must keep your wits about you. There will be plenty of opportunities for champagne and carrying on once you are a married woman. At least until you have a daughter of your own and really know how quickly these negotiations can dissolve, leaving you as hopeless as Ellie Weever. Alone at twenty-two. Working to support *herself*. And the work she does. Preparing bodies for burial." Anna Beth McLeary shivered. "No. That will not happen to you." She straightened the pendant dangling from Bonnie's choker. "Your father gave me this. I hope your husband treats you as well as your father used to treat me."

Anna Beth ran her fingertip over the pendant again then spun Bonnie to glance in the mirror again. "Guests began arriving a bit ago and already your dance card is beginning to fill. I've instructed Mother to distract Mister Ferguson—"

"He's here already?"

"Yes, along with seven others. Several good prospects. One Mother McLeary insisted on inviting that looks as though he'd be more comfortable in the barn than the parlor."

"Oh."

"Yes, I had him sign your card straight away so that you can move on from that obligation quickly."

"Yes, Ma'am."

"Now, I have instructed Mother to distract Mr. Ferguson, Mr. McMaster, and Mr. Baptiste away from signing your card until the last. They are the best ones. Mother McLeary has been assigned the less desirable ones. Hopefully, she can be counted on for this one task and will not suck all the air from the room babbling about your father. *Her* loss. *Her* heartache. As if this has not affected the rest of us."

"Mother, she is grieving her son. She must be so lonely without him."

"We are all lonely. Some of us have been for…But that is not for you to worry about. You my darling, must concentrate on dazzling tonight." Anna Beth McLeary took a step back and gave her daughter a once over, then an approving, albeit thin smile. "I need to get downstairs and keep an eye on Mother McLeary. She kept trying to sneak daffodils into the centerpieces, as if I'm blind. I told her once and for all to stash those heinous yellow things in her room if she must have them, but only lavender crocus will decorate the tables and foyer tonight. A little reminder to these men that you are the flower of spring, the only one they will ever want."

"I hope I am as good to my own daughter as you are to me," Bonnie said with a kiss to her mother's cheek.

"Of course, my dear, you will know exactly what to do," Anna Beth said and crossed to the door, stopping before she opened it. "Tilly will come up and get you when it's time. Do not sit down. That silk will crease no matter how carefully you sit. Come, Tilly."

With that, Bonnie was alone in her bedroom. "So good to see you again, Mister Ferguson," she said and gave her reflection a coy smile. Heat blossomed in her cheeks. "Missus Edward Ferguson.

So good to make your acquaintance." Bonnie extended a down-turned, porcelain hand toward the mirror, giggling at her fantasy. She tilted her chin and raised her gaze to meet her own eyes shining in the glass, just as her mother had taught her. "Oh, Mister Ferguson, you are quite capable with a waltz. My head feels light from the turns." She laughed again, then squared her shoulders. "Why, yes, Mr. Ferguson did recently purchase another hundred acres. We are so blessed."

Bonnie knew she mustn't allow her affection for Edward Ferguson to show, but she had no idea how to hide it. Was she to deny his dark hair, light bronze skin, and eyes nearly as blue as her own? Was she to forget how tall he sat in the saddle as he charged his pony across the polo field? Was she to ignore the sly smile he'd cast her as he sped by that afternoon so many weeks ago or how his smile spread into a grin as his blue eyes locked on hers? Her desire for his rose lips or strong hands was as plain to see as the ball gown she donned.

Two weeks after the annual polo match, which had brought families from as far as one hundred miles, a note from Mr. Edward Ferguson arrived. *Dear Miss McLeary, Thank you for the lovely invitation. I will be delighted to attend your debut. Faithfully, Mr. Edward Ferguson, IV.* Bonnie's mother and grandmothers were aghast at his boldness to address a personal response to Bonnie rather than simply including himself with the family response. But they forgot their disapproval when Bonnie reminded them of the Ferguson fortune.

For forty days and forty nights Edward Ferguson the Fourth became Bonnie's constant obsession. It was his hands Bonnie needed wrapped around her petite waist. For Edward Ferguson's affection alone, she encouraged Tilly to crush her ribs with the boning of her corset. *Faithfully* his. Would he be faithfully hers?

Tilly rapped on the door, barely audible over the sound of the festivities from below and the thundering from beneath Bonnie's breast.

"Yes," Bonnie said, and the door opened. "Is it time?"

Tilly opened the door, nodded, and crossed to Bonnie, still at the mirror.

The time to make her entrance had arrived. Time to make Edward hers. Time to implement the plan crafted with such diligence and cunning that no detail fell unattended. All this done to secure a life filled with security and passion and unplanned joys. Maybe even her unintentional moments were to be blissful. Perhaps she may find a little of the love she now doubted existed between her parents, at least from her mother to her father. Would there be time for that, too? Could she be that blessed?

Tilly with one hand to her chest sighed, a gesture intended to say, "What a lovely young woman." She nodded again then stepped back into the hallway.

At the top of the stairs, Bonnie paused just as her mother had instructed. As the four-piece band played Trumpet Voluntary, Bonnie descended the stairs, feeling Mr. Ferguson's stare but never glancing his way.

⚘

Ellie

NEWS OF THE DEATH spread quickly throughout Huet's Pointe. It moved in whispers across porches and through open parlor windows. Near dusk, it escaped prim lips and landed in Ellie Weever's ear as she walked home from Hodges General Store.

The next morning, Ellie rose early, before dawn, and dressed by lamplight, eager to welcome her guests. With every button of her bodice secured and her apron tied around her slight waist, she carried the lamp from her bedroom, down the stairs, and through the kitchen.

She listened to the ticking of the parlor clock, floating past the furniture and sparse décor of her home. It crept around darkened doorways and over the wooden floor. The sound grew louder against the silence of the house. Troubled by the cadence and the quiet, Ellie walked to the pantry. She was filling her pockets with peppermints when she heard the banging on the death door.

With pale fingers, Ellie slipped a peppermint into her mouth. She tied a handkerchief around her head just below her eyes. The soft, lace edges tickled her chin as she unlocked and pulled open the death door, located off the parlor and never used for any purpose other than to load coffins in and out of the parlor. She sucked on the peppermint while four young, white men and a slender Creole woman, Sabine Fredieu, carried the casket through the door and set it on the table in the center of the parlor.

For nearly an hour, the men leaned against the parlor wall, watching as Ellie and Sabine bathed and dressed the corpse. Ellie could feel their eyes on her, or maybe, they were watching Sabine, the way her petite body rose and fell with every stroke of the washrag.

Already grey with death, the body was filthy. Not just with the evidence of the violent end, but with evidence of how the man had lived. With a wet rag, Ellie wiped the corpse's chest, arms, abdomen, feet, and legs.

"No need for 'im to look perfect," one man leaning against the parlor wall said as Ellie wiped her rag gently across a thigh. "He weren't all that clean when he's alive."

Ellie ignored the comment. She took great care in readying men for burial, even more than the women she had prepared over the last two years. From the moment the death door rattled, Ellie viewed any man in Huet's Point as her own, if only for the short time he lay in her parlor until the widow or mother or daughter appeared to take her man away.

After several more minutes, the corpse lay dressed in a white linen shirt, black trousers, waistcoat, overcoat, and cravat. Although Ellie felt the cravat was a bit fussy for this particular guest, she always abided by the family's wishes. She bent over the casket to fold the corpse's arms over his chest. Her hand tingled when she felt rough calluses rub against her skin.

"You can go now," Ellie said through her kerchief. "I'll finish the preparations."

"Suit yourself," the man standing nearest the death door said. "Guess you'll be needin' these." He reached his own filthy hand toward her and dropped three coins into her hand. "Let's go, Sabine. Boys."

Ellie placed the coins in her pocket and walked the men and Sabine out the front door. Then, she locked the death door. In the kitchen, she scrubbed her hands at the porcelain basin and then rubbed a lavender salve deep into her skin. She retrieved another peppermint from her pocket and sucked air through her nose as the candy melted against her tongue.

With two additional lamps, she returned to the parlor. The sun peeked through the crease of the drawn curtains, but she dared not open them. Ellie couldn't stand the onlookers that gathered on the street in front of her house whenever she worked. And with the rate at which the people of Huet Pointe lined up for their final journey, she could afford all the oil she could burn.

Ellie hoisted the heavy pine lid propped against the table and dragged it into the kitchen. She wouldn't need it again until after the viewing and felt it cluttered the space around her guest. As she pulled it over the lip of the kitchen floor, the wood slipped from her hand and smacked against the floor. She felt a jolt through her entire body as the sound echoed off the high ceilings, hard floors, and uninhabited rooms. The sting of a splinter pulsed in her finger as she walked back into the parlor and sucked harder on the peppermint.

"Well, Ray Don," Ellie said, smiling into the pine box, "let's see what I can do."

Ray Don Lawry, brigand of Huet's Pointe, may have been fresh in the casket, but he definitely didn't look casket fresh. His front was every bit as horrific as the rear view. The bullet entered his left eye, split his skull, and exited out the back of his head. Considering the extent of Ray Don's wound, Ellie thought a simple burial to be best, but Widow Lawry had insisted on a viewing.

"Your lid got me good, Ray Don." Ellie dug her thumbnail into her finger near the splinter and winced as the wooden fleck emerged from beneath her skin. She stuck her finger in her mouth and sucked on the wound for a second. "That was a bad 'ol splinter," she told him, "but I forgive you. I know you didn't mean to hurt me."

Ellie picked up the silver comb from her table of supplies and ran the comb through Ray Don's hair, as if painting gentle strokes on a linen canvas. "I really should thank you, I guess," Ellie said. "Even though it seems awful to thank a man for dyin'. But the

Good Lord provides, Ray Don. Yes, He does. Even if all He's provided me with lately are ne'er-do-wells." Ellie paused and then said with conviction, "Yes, the Lord provides. He brought you to me, and for that, I give thanks."

Ellie stretched the dull brown strands of hair over as much of Ray Don's last moments as possible. After a few minutes, knowing the man didn't have enough hair left to cover the entire wound, she gave up and placed the comb back on the table. She turned back to the casket and caressed Ray Don's good cheek with the back of her fingers. A charge surged through her body as she wondered what his skin felt like before the cold of death.

"You were strong once, weren't you, Ray Don? But tender, too. I bet you could be right tender."

She leaned over the coffin. Little ripples formed on the bridge of her nose beneath the kerchief as she examined the fatal wound. Shaking her head, she told Ray Don, "I just don't think Widow Lawry should have to see that hole in your face." Then Ellie whispered near his ear, "Of course, if'n you ask me, Widow Lawry shouldn't'a took on that name. And before you was dead! That's just bad juju." She pulled another peppermint from her pocket, licked it, and then pulled it into her mouth with her tongue. "A woman ought to be more grateful for a man in her life, 'specially a big, strong man like you." She tilted her head to the side and stared at the wound for several moments, and then, "Oh, I know just what you need!"

Up the stairs in her father's former bedroom, Ellie opened the trunk at the foot of the bed, dressed with a lace-trimmed quilt and linens since her father's death. She sifted through various mementos until she found his collection of eye patches, amassed over his lifetime of caring for the deceased, and chose a plain, black leather patch.

Back in the parlor, she opened her tub of greasepaint. Using an ochre-stained rag she blotted Ray Don's skin with her homemade concoction of lard, cornstarch, and clay until, after several minutes, his complexion didn't look quite so haggard.

"It's a shame to waste good beets on you, Ray Don," Ellie teased as she smashed two fresh beets in a wooden bowl. "But everyone should look their best to meet their maker. I'm just not sure who exactly made you." She dipped one finger into the red beet juice and dabbed Ray Don's cheeks. "Yes, with the devil runnin' through your veins, I wonder if you'd be tender at all. Maybe not," she said and felt the lace of her kerchief tickle her chin again below her playful grin. "Oh, Ray Don, you do tease, don't you?"

The patch would finish Ray Don's burial ensemble. Gently so to avoid the hole in the back of his skull, Ellie lifted the old man's head. "I guess only the Lord knows who killed you, huh? Everybody's talkin' 'bout you and how the perfect shot that brought you down, but nobody's saying who did you in." Ray Don's face grazed her bosom as she wrapped the strap around his head just above his ears and positioned the patch over his left eye. For the third time that morning, her body prickled with longing. "It's just a cryin' shame to come to such a vicious end, Ray Don. Just a cryin' shame."

Ellie shook her head and then straightened Ray Don's shirt collar. She retrieved the three pennies from her pocket and balanced one coin on Ray Don's lips and one on his right eye. After a moment of contemplation while rubbing the third coin between two fingers, she closed her hand around it. "I guess you cain't see outta that left eye no ways. You don't mind, do you, dearest?"

Content with Ray Don's appearance, she glanced at the clock centered on the mantle. Ray Don's final preparations ate up most of the time Ellie had hoped to use preparing herself for the viewing. In a rush, she tossed her combs, greasepaint, bowls, brushes, and rags in the leather satchel on the floor near the table and picked up the bowl of smashed beets. Then she blew out the lamps and went to the kitchen where she scrubbed her hands clean a second time. Back in the parlor, she pulled the curtains open. Sunlight flooded the room and cast a warm glow on Ray Don's face.

"God bless you, Ray Don," Ellie said, as she wrapped her fingers around the stiff handle of her leather satchel and admired her latest creation. "And if He cain't do that, maybe He'll have mercy on your soul."

In her bedroom, she placed the penny from her pocket on her vanity, set the satchel on the floor just inside the door, and quickly undressed. Her frock and apron she threw into a heap on the floor and then slipped into her favorite funeral attire: long, black silk with a fitted waist and high lace collar over several starched petticoats. She glided around her bedroom for a moment and listened to the swish of the layers. Glancing at her reflection in the bubbled mirror, she stopped and pinched her cheeks. *Maybe today*, she thought to herself. Viewings for notorious no-gooders like Ray Don Lawry attracted every farmer, merchant, and fisherman across the bayou. *Maybe today.*

As long as the people of Huet's Pointe kept her in business she didn't need a husband, at least not financially, but she still held out hope that one day she would no longer suck on peppermint or spread lye from the kitchen to the parlor and up the stairs or dig splinters from pine boxes out of her fingers or scrub her hands raw four times a day or listen to the silence of the house. She could leave the curtains open and move the china hutch from the dining room to the parlor and block the death door forever, and really know what a man, his warm skin, callused hands and broad shoulders felt like.

"Ellie Weever," Widow Lawry yelled from downstairs. "Get your rear end down here, now!" Maggie Lawry had always had a way of making her presence known. With her husband dead and almost buried, no one remained to temper her behavior, not that Ray Don was ever any good at that.

Startled, Ellie grabbed the penny from her dresser and stashed it in the hidden pocket of her full skirt. "Widow Lawry," Ellie called from the landing, "is there a problem?"

"What the hell is on his face?" Widow Lawry asked, pointing one sausage-like finger inches from Ray Don's nose as Ellie rushed into the parlor.

"An eye patch, ma'am. I thought it best to cover the wound."

"Well, you thought wrong." Then Widow Lawry snatched the coins off his eyes and lips. "And he won't be needin' these where he's goin'." She extended her hand, palm up, to Ellie. "I know my idiot boy gave you three when he dropped off the old buzzard. Where's the third?"

Ellie took the third coin from her pocket and gave it to the widow. Embarrassed, she avoided Widow Lawry's gaze.

"Now you fix him right!" Widow Lawry shoved the coins into the crease between the two ample breasts threatening to escape her bodice.

"Ma'am?" Ellie asked, taken aback by Maggie's harsh tone and offensive attire.

Pointing again at the eye patch, Widow Lawry demanded, "You take that thing off him right now."

Ellie leaned over Ray Don and carefully removed the patch as Maggie bent over the coffin, so close to Ellie that the widow's skirt brushed against her own. The dowager's hot, foul breath, like sulfur gas rising from the swamp, coated Ellie's neck in noxious fumes. She swore the stench lingered in her hair as she slipped one hand into her pocket, digging for a third peppermint. Her pocket was empty, so she held her breath as she removed the eye patch from Ray Don's face.

"That's better," whispered Maggie, and then with pride, "now everyone can see the shot that finally put the bastard down."

Ellie looked into Maggie's eyes, surprised by the absence of grief.

"You're a smart girl, Ellie Weever, not to marry. Husbands only bring you trouble."

"Yes, ma'am," Ellie told the widow. "If you'll excuse me, I need a moment." Ellie nodded quickly and then walked back up the stairs, aching to be anywhere but near Maggie Lawry.

Alone in her bedroom, she grabbed a peppermint from the pocket of the skirt she'd left heaped on the floor. She thought of Maggie Lawry's dark eyes as she examined the candy and removed a fleck of lint from it.

"She's wrong," Ellie whispered. "I am not meant to be alone."

She popped the peppermint into her mouth and bit down, grinding her teeth into the sugar. *Maybe today*, she thought again. *Maybe today.*

✧

Coraline and Lulu

CORALINE DURAND DIDN'T NOTICE the woman staring at her from below the fat branch. With her tiptoes planted against one branch and leaning on her elbows on another, Coraline stared through her Grandmama's opera glasses, lifted from the old lady's bureau for one imperative purpose—eavesdropping. The pint-size peeper had to get a glimpse of an honest-to-God outlaw, even if he was soon-to-be maggot food. From her hiding place in the large oak across the street from Ellie Weever's house, Huet Pointe's only funeral parlor, Coraline had a clear shot through the parlor window to Ray Don Lawry, bloated has-been in a pine box.

"See anything good?" Lulu Dann asked, tilting her large purple hat toward the sky to peer at the girl in the giant oak with a base so wide a family of four could live in its trunk. "As for me, I got a clear shot up that dress of yours."

"That's uncalled for," Coraline said, her cheeks and neck a sudden bright pink. She smacked at her skirts in an attempt to hide her unmentionables. In the fuss over skirts and modesty – both ridiculous in Coraline's mind – Grandmama's opera glasses slipped through Coraline's fingers. A hushed gasp escaped Coraline's lips as she watched her stolen prize plummet toward the ground.

With one lacey hand, Lulu caught the glasses. She turned them over, admiring the ivory and emerald tulips embedded in royal blue enamel on the bell-shaped binoculars. "These must've cost a pretty penny. Definitely did not come from ol' Hodges General."

"Those are mine," Coraline said, swinging down from the branch, then the next. Like a cat, she landed on two, soft feet right in front of Lulu. "You can give them back now."

"Well, now, I don't know if I should do that." Lulu twirled the glasses out of Coraline's reach with the engraved handle. Little specks of sunshine danced off the green jewels and brass frame. "How do I know these actually belong to you? Maybe I should get Sheriff Tuckey over here. I'm sure he's inside." Lulu gestured across the street at Ellie Weever's house.

"Those are mine. Well, my Grandmama's..."

"Now, we get the truth. Does *Grandmama* know you're climbing trees out here, peeking through windows with her fancy scope?"

"Scope? You don't even know what they are. *Those* are opera glasses. Give them back. Now." Coraline reached out her small, bare hand.

"Oh-oh. Grandmama likes the opera, huh?" Lulu stooped a bit to be eye level with Coraline. "Young lady, it don't matter if I know what the proper name of something is. I know what emeralds look like, and I know what stolen looks like."

"I just borrowed them. I'm gonna put 'em back." Coraline felt the flush come back to her cheeks, but this time it wasn't embarrassment, but rather panic. The threat of the Ursuline Academy in New Orleans was one of her grandmother's favorites. Under the shade of that giant oak, Coraline began to fear that life in a convent of jagged-nosed, thick-knuckled nuns was a distinct possibility. "Please. Please don't do that." Coraline fought back the fearful tears pooling in her eyes.

"Here ya go, honey." Lulu handed the glasses to Coraline. "I was just teasing with you. Trust me, Sheriff Tuckey and I aren't close."

Coraline removed a handkerchief from her cuff and wrapped the glasses, securing them in the ruffled pocket of her pinafore. "Thank you."

Lulu glanced across the street. "Are you going inside, or are you more of just a looky-loo?"

"Are you?"

"A looky-loo? Nah. I like to be in the action rather than tucked away."

"No," Coraline giggled at the purple lady's teasing. "Are you going into the viewing?"

"Absolutely. I've a vested interest in making sure that man is dead." Lulu held up one hand and folded back an empty lace finger of her glove.

"You're missing a finger!" Coraline nearly fell to the ground as she jumped backward, away from the woman, petite in stature but made bigger by her impressive hat, bold attitude, and gross disfigurement.

"Very astute," Lulu sneered. "It's nothing to be afraid of – just a nub."

"Were you one of Mr. Lawry's victims?" Coraline's arms pimpled as she stared at the lacey nub.

"First and foremost, Lulu Dann isn't anyone's victim. Secondly, you can call that bastard Ray Don. He doesn't deserve your pleasantries. But, yes, you could say he put into action the course of events that led to me losing most of this here finger."

Coraline swallowed hard when she realized the identity of the purple lady: Lulu Dann of Dann's Hall and Saloon. Lulu Dann, the new top whore of Huet Pointe. Lulu Dann, the woman who, when Grandmama caught Coraline eavesdropping in the hallway as the high society fuddle-duddies gossiped about her over tea one afternoon, caused her to receive five lashings and a week's worth of a tender rear-end. Lulu Dann, whose words were as colorful and twisted as any book Coraline had ever read.

"I guess along with *borrowing* Grandmama's things without permission, you also shouldn't be talking to me? Or am I misinterpreting that look on your face?"

"No, ma'am, I just…well, Grandmama said what you do is…" Coraline hesitated. She didn't want to outright call the woman a sinner. She knew that wasn't right. To outright call a person a sinner. But what should she call a woman who does what she does? But, on the other hand, the woman was unlike any woman she'd ever met. This woman, Lulu Dann, spoke to her as a real person – not a child, not a thing to be pitied or disciplined or sheltered – but a real person.

"A sin?" Lulu asked.

"Yes." Coraline bowed her head, hating the word no matter how honest her answer and the fact that she'd been taught to always, always, always be honest or risk the strap.

"Ain't no shame in calling a thing what it is," Lulu told the girl. "But there is shame in sneaking around. Hiding in trees and peeking through fancy spectacles through other people's windows." Lulu stared down at Coraline, waiting for an answer that did not come. "So, Miss Looky-loo, what do you say for yourself?"

Coraline glanced back, unsure of how to answer. The truth was far from interesting.

"Why don't you start with your name?"

"Coraline. Coraline Durand."

"Oh. So…" Lulu's face softened, but only for a second. To Coraline's relief any pity Lulu may have felt passed. "So, why, Miss Coraline Durand, were you up in that tree peeking through that window?"

Coraline sucked in, then blurted the words out before she could change her mind. "Just to get a look at somebody who did whatever he wanted whenever he wanted without any consequences."

"There's always consequences, kid."

"Not for him there wasn't!"

"I say a bullet to the face is a pretty stark consequence."

"But before that. Imagine it. Mr. La…I mean Ray Don wasn't scared of anyone, so everyone was scared of him. He just made up his own way of doing things. Mama used to tell me stories of him and his gang. Running around. Thieving. Taking whatever they wanted, when they wanted. Then they'd get back to their secret hideout and dance and hoot and holler at the moon till the sun came up. I heard he even went out to Pirate Island and took on all those nasty men himself. Stole all their gold! Mama also told me that he used to wrestle gators and he'd train 'em like watchdogs at their hideout…"

"Honey, honey, honey," Lulu pressed her hand against her stomach as if her laughter threatened the seams of her corset. No one had made her bust a gut like that in weeks. Possibly ever. "Your mama sounds like one heck of a storyteller." Lulu glanced toward Ellie Weever's large Colonial again. The front porch had a steady stream of mourners, or at least voyeurs and gossips running across it. "All right, now, I've got to go in there real quick. Just to make sure he's good and gone. Maybe whoever did it is in there holdin' court so I can thank him. Or her?" Lulu flashed a wicked grin at Coraline – one that thrilled the child. "Will you be here when I come out? You can climb back up in that tree and wait if you prefer."

"Yes, Ma'am. I'll be here."

"Ma'am? Why, I never. Must be the new hat." Lulu adjusted the large chiffon bow on her hat so that the brim tilted just so, and then crossed the street.

Mamba Loo would've smacked her lips at the purple hat while Grandmama recited a diatribe against tacky displays, vanity, and pride, with a few versus of Latin thrown in for good measure. But not Coraline. She had a new goal in life: To one day don a hat wider than her shoulders but angled to shade only half her face.

Then, when she crossed the street, the world would get out of her way.

When Lulu emerged from the house, descending the front porch steps like the Queen of England, the purple hat her crown, Coraline sat on the ground beneath the tree. She'd found the perfect depression in the trunk where the bark had only soft edges and waited in plain sight.

"No hiding this time around?" Lulu asked as she approached. "Well, come on then." Lulu walked with an intentional stride past the tree.

Coraline stood and stutter-stepped to catch Lulu. Within a few minutes, they stood side-by-side before the open water of the bayou.

"This bay leads somewhere, you know." With one hand—the one with the nub—Lulu loosened her hatpin. She removed her hat and closed her eyes. The spring wind, cool and bright, blew against her face, freeing a few tendrils of dark auburn hair. "I know it looks like the water is only coming towards us, but as sure as the waves beat against this dock, they also flow out. Out, out, out. Far away from here."

"Uh huh." Coraline didn't appreciate the prattling of adults – misty eyed in deep thought, sure the listener was changed forever by their words of wisdom. *Blah, blah, blah.*

"Ray Don Lawry could have gone anywhere he wanted. He had the means to, you know, but he decided to stay around here." With her full skirt rocking back and forth – a big, purple bell in a breeze - Lulu glanced behind her at an empty bench. She sauntered over and sat. "I could've gone anywhere I wanted, but I stayed. Do you know why?"

"Because this is your home?"

"Goodness no. I don't have a home, not in the real sense. People care about you and for you, so you care about the place, wherever your people call home. I've got no people, so I've got no home. Especially this place."

"Well, it *is* where you live." Coraline sat on the bench, hip-to-hip with Lulu Dann.

Lulu glanced at the child, amused by her matter-of-fact way of speaking. Too many adults spoke in crafted circles. Lulu even found herself falling into the Huet Pointe code. "Yes, this is where I live, so in a physical sense it is home, but I chose to stay in this Godforsaken town because this is where I have something of my own. Mine. No one can take it away or tell me what to do with it."

"Bully for you," Coraline said and fingered the opera glasses tucked in her pockets.

"As much as I hate him and his whole gang of bastards and that demon of a wife of his, the same was true for Ray Don. He carved out something of his own here. Of course, some argue he did that with other people's belongings." Lulu paused, tripped up for a moment by the philosophical debate. "Anywho. Everybody has to have something of their own. And they got to feel like they got what they earned. And they wanted what they got."

Coraline slipped her hand inside her pocket and pressed her fingertips against the glasses. Even through the handkerchief wrapping, she could feel the raised edges of the emeralds, the very same green of her eyes. This time, though, Lulu saw Coraline's feeling of the glasses and noticed the child's crestfallen expression.

"So, you think you've nothing of your own? Surely something in that big ol' house you live in is yours."

"You might think that, but..."

"Well, I know you don't own your own fancy scope," Lulu laughed. "So, no armoire full of pretty dresses and drawers full of bonnets, each with a pair of matching gloves?"

"Of course, I have those," Coraline said in protest, but Lulu kept talking.

"No dollhouse to waste away the hours arranging furniture and pretending the people inside is real?"

"Yes, I've got one of those, but I don't…"

"No dollies in pretty pink dresses and ruffled bassinette?"

Coraline's face flushed to a hot pink. Perhaps she didn't like Lulu Dann as much as she first thought. Perhaps Miss Dann was just another adult to throw her weight around. "Of course…"

"Sounds like you got all sorts of your own things."

Coraline stood and faced the woman wearing so much purple she had begun to morph into a big blob of grape jam. Coraline ripped at the bows in her hair, tied one to each of the braided pigtails hanging six inches below each square shoulder. She tossed the bows in Lulu's lap. "Do I look like I want to play with dollies and fake houses and wear all these ruffles and bows? Do you think I consider any of this mine?"

"Now we're getting somewhere!" Lulu leaned forward on the bench, so close to Coraline she could smell the sweet citrus of the little girl's soap. "If they're not yours, whose are they?"

"Grandmama's!"

Two fishermen dripping wet and slimed with bayou scum and fish guts stopped short two jetties over, turned and glared at the little girl. "You two hens are scarin' away the fish," one yelled.

"Your stink is scarin' away the fish," Lulu snapped back.

"Shut your trap or move on," the fisherman ordered.

Lulu stood. She shaded her eyes against the noon sun with her nub hand. "Bartholomew Tindle, I know you are not speaking to me with that tone!"

Even from a hundred feet away, the blush on his cheeks shone clear over to the bench, Coraline, and Lulu.

"That's right, Mr. Tindle, and I get to be as loud as I want to. So does my new friend. Now, you just go on 'bout your business. And you better think good and long about how you want to apologize to me." With one fist planted on her hip, Lulu grinned at the man. "See you Friday next, Barty."

Coraline had witnessed Grandmama berate the servants; criticize the maids for the inadequate shine on the floor or the venison being too chewy. Mamba Loo had on several occasions voiced her opinions and criticisms and barked orders at the cooks, the female field hands, and the scullery maids. But, never in Coraline's life had she seen a woman command respect from a man in the way that Lulu Dann did just then. Coraline's mother had tried, and that attempt at respect had led to her being murdered in her own parlor. From that moment, Coraline figured men made the rules and women followed the rules or snuck around them. Is it possible she was wrong?

With the scuttlebutt over, Lulu sat again and patted the empty space next to her. "Here, try this." Lulu handed Coraline the purple hat.

"But that's your hat. And it goes so perfectly with your dress."

"Honey, I ain't giving it to you to keep. I handed it to you to try on. You can't have anything of your own until you figure out what it is you want. Now, go on, try it. Maybe it'll feel better than Grandmama's bows."

Coraline donned the wide-brimmed, amethyst hat. She felt of the hat with both hands, straightening the bow and tipping up the brim as best she could without the benefit of a mirror. "How does it look," Coraline asked. But, as she stood and turned to Lulu, Grandmama stopped short at the shore end of the dock. Coraline swallowed hard against a panic surging up from her stomach into her cheeks.

Lulu followed the child's wide eyes, rotating on the bench so that she could glance behind her. "That must be Grandmama."

"Yes." Coraline tried to move her feet but the fear in every last one of her cells had turned her to stone – a little girl statue in a gigantic purple hat.

"Coraline Durand, you take that off right this instant." Grand-mama barreled over the planks of the pier. "And get away from that trollop!"

"Now's your chance, honey. Grab it before it's gone." Lulu stood next to Coraline. "You got to tell people what you want. And, if she don't listen, tell her again."

"I've never been so embarrassed in my life," Grandmama said, jerking Coraline by the arm as soon as she was within snatching distance. The old lady tore the purple hat off Coraline's head and threw it at Lulu. "Having Ernestine Harris rush up to me while I'm keeping adoration for Ray Don Lawry's burning soul and tell me she saw *my* granddaughter walking to the dock with this piece of swamp trash!"

"Grandmama, we were just talking."

"I can see that. Now listen to me, you've got nothing to say to her kind. Not a word."

"My kind?" Lulu remarked as she fastened her hat back on her head, twirling two tendrils around her finger so they bounced against her cheekbone and ear upon release. "Perhaps she shouldn't be talking to *my kind*, but believe you me, that girl has plenty to say. Perhaps you should start listening."

"I will not stand her before God Almighty and half the fish-ermen of Huet Pointe," Grandmama sneered, waving her arm toward the nearly empty dock, "and listen to a woman like you tell me what a young lady needs." With that, Grandmama turned, yanking Coraline along the dock toward the beaten grass path that led them home. Coraline was quite sure the path also led to the strap or maybe Grandmama would live up to her promise of taking a choice, thorny switch from Ernestine Harris' rose bushes.

One week later, in the second to last car of Smoky Mary, chug-ging along the final bit of track from Huet Pointe to New Orleans, Coraline Durand shifted in her seat. Try as she might, twisting to this position or that, the hard leather seat was no comfort to her blistered bottom. Ten lashings were doled out not five minutes after her Grandmama dragged her through the front door and into the parlor. Coraline swore she saw a smile crack the old crow's face as the strap came down for the final blow.

From the station just east of the French Quarter, a place Coraline dreamt of exploring, a carriage and chaperone would escort her ten miles outside of the city proper. There, an Ursuline Sister, a black and white statue of piety and obedience, would lead Coraline through the gates of the convent, then behind the walls intended to encase her for the next three months—the remainder of the spring semester, paid in full. Coraline imagined the smile that cracked Grandmama's wrinkles as she counted out the notes.

Well, the joke's on her, Coraline mused, her anxiety eased by the rocking of the train. Even as it listed around curves, the train seemed to promise a new balance in Coraline's life.

After what could only be described as a feverish, maddened lashing, Grandmama dragged Coraline to the pump behind the kitchen. There, in earshot of every butler, maid, and field hand of the Durands, Grandmama held Coraline's head under the ice-cold water. She dug her brittle nails into the child's scalp, screaming of lice and disease. The lye soap sizzled against the fresh cuts in her scalp. Coraline yelped and begged for mercy, but still Grandmama scrubbed. Then, when the old lady was spent, satisfied that nothing of the whore remained on Coraline, Grandmama retired for the day. She took dinner in her private quarters, claiming the day had been too taxing on her nerves to leave the confines of her bedchamber. She did, however, have the wherewithal to write Coraline a note:

Pack your trunk. You may take one day dress, one evening dress, the necessary accompaniments, one dressing gown, and one pair of boots. Pack your underthings and toilet case. Neither Mamba Loo nor I will assist you, as you've broken both our hearts.

As soon as Coraline saw the words *pack* and *trunk*, she knew she was headed for the Ursuline Academy with its required, drab uniform, formal study in French, English, stationery, and needle-work, and the suffocating confines of convent walls. The best she could say of the Ursuline nuns was that they spoke, unlike many of the cloistered orders dotting the infantile map of the southern United States.

That evening, after a supper of crusted bread, cheese, and pickled beets, which Grandmama knew Coraline hated, the little girl sat outside her grandmother's door. Coraline waited until she was sure she heard the labored breathing of old nasal passages. Convinced the old bat was sound asleep, Coraline darted back to her own bedroom, flung open the window, and shimmied down the tree.

Twenty minutes later she stood at the kitchen door of the House of Dann, gambling hall and saloon. The clanking and dinging of a harpsichord flooded the alleyway. She knocked hard against the door, so hard she was sure she bruised her knuckles.

A man in grease-stained shirt and apron answered the door, shocked at the sight of a young girl.

"I need to see Miss Lulu Dann. Please. It's urgent."

A few minutes later, Lulu flung open the door, nearly spilling into the alleyway, and glanced at the child with foggy eyes. "What the hell are you doing here?"

"She's sending me away. To the nuns. She's sending me away." Rivers of tears and snot streaked Coraline's face.

"Lord, you're a mess." Lulu took a long swig of the brown liquid sloshing around in her crystal highball. "The girls and me just doing a bit of celebrating on account of that bastard Ray Don and that big 'ol hole in his face. Care to join us?" Lulu laughed, loud and ugly, then stumbled as she stepped on the hem of her dress, still purple but rumpled from wear.

"No. I don't care to join you. Didn't you hear me? She's sending me away!"

Lulu stared at the girl for several moments, breathing in and out so that a cloud of scotch smacked Coraline in the face. "What do you 'spect me to do? We all got our troubles, Miss Cor-line Duran'." Then, Lulu turned from the girl and toddled back through the kitchen and out of sight.

With the door swung open, Coraline turned and ran. Without thought, her feet carried her back home and up the tree and through the window to her bedroom where Mamba Loo startled her, sitting on her bed.

"What are you doing in here?" Coraline asked and walked to the vanity. "You can go ahead and tell Grandmama I snuck out again. Ain't a thing more she can do to me today." Coraline splashed water from the basin onto her face.

"Now, Baby Girl, why would I do that?"

"Because you both hate me. You're against me just like she is."

"Child, I couldn't hate you if I tried. I don't agree with some of your wild goings on, but I could never hate you."

"Then why are you mad at me? All I did was talk to that woman."

"I'm not mad at you. I'm mad at your grandmother. She got no sense."

"Then stop her. Don't let her send me away."

"Child, after what all she did to you today, I can't let her keep you. She don't deserve you."

"Grandmama says I broke your heart."

"The only part of me that's sad is the part that's gonna miss you." Mamba Loo took the girl in her arms and held her against her soft body. She stroked the child's back as tears soaked through her blouse and onto her black skin. "You go on and cry now, and when you're done, we gonna get you ready for your new start. Far away from this town and everybody in it causes you pain."

A new start. A new beginning. Springtime along the Mississippi. Coraline watched through the window as they approached the station. She breathed in and out and didn't care that the air was thick with foreign, pungent smells and humidity akin to mashed potatoes. She was far from Huet Pointe and Grandmama and any reminders of who she was before.

No more adults calling her a child and a liar, accusing her of not understanding or making up stories. No one dressing her up in ruffles and bows that made her want to peel off her own skin. Ruffles and bows were only allowed within the walls of Ursuline on rare occasions. She could just blend in with all the other orphan girls, the other pitied souls and left-behinds. Be around *her kind*. Breathe again. *Breathe*.

𑀫

Part Five

Another Summer in That Damned Spot

WHITE, FRAYED TENTACLES stretched across a bright blue sky. Mamba Loo had awoken early that morning as she always did. But, in that June dawn, she'd prayed to her Iwa and to God Almighty that her restless sleep would prove wrong. The cerulean sky did little to comfort her as the clouds inched closer to Huet Pointe.

Mamba Loo spoke few words on her walk to the McLeary Plantation. If she had been in the mood to talk, she could barely have gotten a word in over the chattering of the trees—the debate between the pine, oak, and cypress was heated. In addition, of course, were the excited ramblings of nearly all of Huet Pointe's cooks, butlers, and maids. The day would be unlike any other Huet Pointe had known. Visitors from the northeast had arrived the previous evening. Two stagecoaches of actors and two of costumes, props, and set dressing had been loaded onto barges for the final crossing. Anyone who was anyone in Huet Pointe, along with those who weren't, had gathered at the dock to watch them float into their small hamlet. A grand spectacle indeed and merely the pre-show.

Huet Pointe would be host to the troubadours and had every intention to do it up right. From Hodges Store to the one café to the small, white church, the town buzzed. Even the girls at the House of Dann Hall and Saloon replaced their typical snark with an air of delight. So, who could keep silent on a day such as this?

Mamba Loo could, for if she spoke, she feared madness would escape her lips. Surely that was what she'd heard — madness.

So she walked, jogged really, catching joyful half-mutterings from the stream of borrowed help. The voices clanged against each other, interrupting, changing keys and meter, obstructing Mamba Loo's ears and understanding. If only they would be silent for a moment so an old woman could think.

"I hope we get to see some of it," Sabine chirped as she tried in vain to keep up with Mamba Loo, leading the river of servants through the sugarcane. "Do you think they will let us? Miz McLeary that is. Do you think she will let us watch?" Sabine's employer, Marguerite Lawry, now officially the Widow Lawry, had offered Sabine to Anna Beth McLeary for the day in exchange for an invitation. "Maybe I will be able to peek in from the back. That wouldn't disturb anyone, now, would it?"

Mamba Loo stared at the young woman, wondering what she'd asked or said. But the old oak of a woman didn't stop or listen or question Sabine or to tell her to stop yapping and trifling over plays and all that nonsense. In that moment, Mamba Loo knew she had failed Sabine in her study of the Nago. The girl was still unable to hear the trees, still unencumbered by knowledge. Mamba Loo envied Sabine's ignorance.

"Just you wait. You're going to love it, Mamba," Sabine told her. "Sister Angelique lent me a copy of the play when I was at the convent. I must have read it a hundred times before Mother Superior found it in my room and took it away. She said it wasn't appropriate for a girl my age or any Christian girl at all. So, that tells you it must be good, right?"

Mamba Loo squinted at Sabine a final time before dashing through the sugarcane. The fields gave way to McLeary Plantation proper. Mamba skirted slave shacks and stables then went straight through the manicured gardens. Up, up, up the stairs to the back porch. Around one corner and another. Through opposing rows of perfectly white rocking chairs. At last, Mamba gripped the iron handle and swung open the servant's entrance. She closed the door tight behind her, sweating from the effort.

"What on earth? Mamba Loo, open this door," Sabine insisted.

"Oh, oh, honey," Mamba Loo said, allowing Sabine entrance to the mudroom. "I didn't realize." Mamba pushed the door closed behind Sabine. Respite from the trees was necessity. She had to block their merciless rantings.

"You don't seem to be realizin' much of anything this morning." Sabine reached her hands behind her back to re-tie her apron.

"You's one of the prettiest faces I've ever seen, Sabine." Mamba Loo stared into Sabine's eyes as she spoke the heavy-hearted compliment.

"You're as strange as a five-legged toad this morning, Mamba. Somebody cast a spell on you for a change?" Sabine giggled as she walked away to explore the mansion. The cavernous hallways leading this way and that of the McLeary mansion called to her. She'd never seen such true wealth. Oh, sure, the Lawry's had money, stolen money, *new* money. And as is often the truth with something new, the novice owner had no idea what to do with it.

The McLearys, on the other hand, were old hat with money. Every inch of the mansion displayed a skill of what to do with profits from the sugarcane trade. The ceilings floated at twelve feet, far out of Sabine's reach. Each room crowned with at least one oil-burning, crystal chandelier. Embossed wallpaper covered the walls. Sabine reached out a hand and ran her fingertips over the raised floral design. For a moment she wondered why Madam McLeary bothered to hang artwork. The family portraits and still life paintings of Angel's Trumpets seemed unnecessary when the wallpaper was itself art.

"Don't let the McLearys find you nosin' 'round in here," Mamba Loo warned Sabine after she crossed the vast foyer and through the mauve-coated parlor. "Ain't none of 'em kind 'cept for

Bonnie. Three mean old hens all trapped under one roof, the rest of 'em is. Each one with a sharper peck than the other." Mamba Loo ushered Sabine around two round settees and between the pocket doors that lead into the dining room.

"This is where they take their meals?" Sabine spun around taking in the lavish space. "The ceiling looks to be on fire!" She grinned at the hammered copper ceiling above her head. Three chandeliers, one hanging above the center then two at each end of a twenty-foot-long mahogany table, sprayed refracted light around the room.

"You best act like you seen such before," Mamba Loo told Sabine. "Or like you don't see a thing a-tal. Now hush."

Sabine and Mamba Loo took their place in the throng—the river of white and black garb on black and brown skin had resting along the walls of the dining room. Sabine pressed her lips shut and forced herself to stare at the floor, also spectacular in its high shine but blessedly lacking ornate amusements.

All fell silent as a black butler with trimmed salt and pepper hair and tailoring that rivaled any plantation master crossed through the massive doors. He strutted down the line of borrowed help, examining with great efficiency every detail of his temporary staff. Near the hearth, he addressed the crowd. "We's got a ton to do 'fore all these guests arrive. So, if you know your assignment, get to it. If not, come see me and I'll place you. Best not let me catch you dilly dallying 'round. I ain't afraid to use the whip."

"We're on polish," Mamba Loo told Sabine and dragged her by the arm to the far side of the table. "I's worked it out last week with Tilly—that's Miz McLeary's girl."

"I know who Tilly is, Mamba," Sabine said, confused again by Mamba Loo's behavior. "You surely are peculiar today."

"Just polish," Mamba Loo said and handed Sabine a soft, white cloth retrieved from her pocket. "Nobody needs to run they mouths whiles they polish."

Mamba picked one saucer up off a tall stack of gold-trimmed china and began rubbing her own cloth against the gold rim. She had a clear shot through the center picture window to the tree line. There, she decided, she would polish plates, saucers, bowls, and silver until her joints ached, out of earshot of the damned trees.

With the late day sun glowing a dim orange, guests arrived, packing the McLeary foyer, parlor, and dining room. They lingered in hallways and gossiped along verandas.

The play would be unlike anything they'd ever seen—a tragedy rich in violence and suspense, or so Grandmama told Mamba Loo when she'd asked a week prior what a *Macbeth* was. Grandmama had wrinkled her nose and let out an indignant harrumph when Mamba Loo had inquired about the play. "Macbeth tells of the dangers of ambition, of setting aside morality to achieve selfish goals. Your kind wouldn't understand. It's all very complex."

Mamba Loo had allowed the insult, knowing the delight Grandmama took in being the smartest in the room. Coraline's absence had done nothing to cool the old bag's temper; it only removed her favorite target.

For that reason, Mamba left the skinniest of the skinny maids with Grandmama that morning. Madam Durant had insisted she could care for herself, but Mamba knew as soon as the old woman was forced to prepare her own noon meal, hefty consequences would be rendered. Mamba Loo set the lunch tray just as Grandmama preferred, had one of the field hands kill and clean a chicken, then instructed the skinny girl how to fry it without burning the kitchen to the ground. Then, she rushed out the door and into a cacophony—the trees impatient and irate.

"You should be ashamed of yourself," Mother McLeary whispered to Anna Beth. The two widows stood hip-to-hip near the grand staircase as more guests crossed the threshold. "I knew you were never good enough for my Gil, but tonight you've outdone yourself."

"Please mark Miz Dann as arrived, Tilly," Anna Beth, ignoring her mother-in-law, told her maid. Tilly responded with a quick scratch of charcoal through the name Madam Lulu Dann then folded the worn paper and tucked it in her apron pocket. "This will work, Tilly. It's going to work."

"Because honoring what Gil spent his too-short life building would be...what, Anna Beth? Terrible? Too much for you to handle? Or, perhaps, unworthy of your precious time and effort?"

"You are welcome to choose any of those very sound reasons, Mother McLeary." Anna Beth peered through the assemblage and found her daughter. She smiled at Bonnie who stood next to her prize, the dashing Edward Ferguson, heir to the Ferguson cotton fortune. Mobile, Alabama, was not Anna Beth's beloved Richmond, Virginia, but it would be a far cry better than the moldy drain that was Huet Pointe. Anna Beth, to her mind, had tried to smell the roses and honeysuckles and even her precious Angel's Trumpet. None showed her a sweeter side of Huet Pointe.

"I will never know why Gil was so devoted to you," Mother McLeary said, practically seizing with disappointment, and dabbed the corner of her mouth with a lace handkerchief. The stress of Gil's death ate away at her stomach lining resulting in drops of blood escaping her esophagus and into her mouth. "He built all of this for you, and now you intend to give it away to the highest bidder? Even if that bidder is a whore? She will turn this place into a brothel, and you know it."

"If selling this place will satisfy the Fergusons so that Bonnie marries well, then yes," Anna Beth turned to her mother-in-law, removing any space for civility between them. Through clenched teeth she insisted, "I will sell it to a priest, a whore, a rogue, to Lucifer himself!"

"My son would never allow such trash as Lulu Dann into his home!"

"Your darling boy laid down with that trash at least twice a week." Anna Beth's tone cooled as she landed her final blow. Then, the hostess turned on her heels and glided down the hall, smiling and nodding at guests until she reached her sweet Bonnie.

"Tilly," Mother McLeary said as she turned from the guests, "please send for me when the play is to start. I must lie down for a bit. My daughter-in-law doesn't…" A coughing spree sent her down the hall and up the back stairs without another coherent word. Later, two sips from her half-ounce bottle of Laudanum along with strict orders from Anna Beth to Tilly to, "Let the damned crow sleep," would prevent Mother McLeary from rejoining the festivities.

Around the corner in the dining room, Ellie Weever nibbled a shrimp puff as she eyed an open seat on the second row, fighting a heated yet internal battle: Reserve a seat by placing her gloves on the cushion or wait for guidance from the hostess.

"Madam McLeary knew who would be attending. Why wouldn't she use place cards?" Ellie asked aloud before she realized who'd approached her.

"That's not the custom. Have you never been to a play before?" Ernestine Harris asked.

"Once, but I was very young. Daddy took us to New Orleans for two whole weeks. Magical place."

"If you can stomach the smell," Rosarie Hodges giggled as she glided up, coming to a swaying stop on Ernestine's right.

"Perhaps you should let the next round of champagne pass you by, Rosarie." Ernestine motioned to Rosarie's half-full flute.

"Miss, yes you," Ellie Weever called to Sabine who balanced a cocktail tray of hors d'oeuvres, weaving around layered skirts and bronze-backed, dining chairs. "Yes, come, please." Then, in an attempt to keep the evening conflict-free, said, "Rosarie, you simply must try the shrimp puffs. They are divine. Bonnie told me her mother scoured over the menu for two whole weeks. Not a single detail overlooked. Well, except place settings, which would have been thoughtful," said Ellie with a sideways glare at Ernestine.

"I heard," Ernestine whispered as Sabine held out the tray for the women to sample a few, "that this is all a ruse to convince someone to buy this place. It came to me on good authority that Gil acquired quite the debt building Anna Beth and Bonnie this estate. Then I heard that Mister Ferguson, Bonnie's betrothed, wants nothing to do with this land or Mister McLeary's debt. If Anna Beth can't find a buyer before the wedding date, the marriage is off."

"How terrible," Rosarie chirped.

Ellie glared at Ernestine, as if slapped with the realization that she had consorted with the enemy who had executed quite the ambush. "You shouldn't gossip like that. It isn't right and what you are saying simply cannot be true. Bonnie would have told me if her engagement was in jeopardy or contingent upon selling her family home. She would have confided in me." Ellie tossed her linen napkin on Sabine's tray (ruining two puffs as they deflated under the weight) and bolted across the room.

Sabine peered over her shoulder, watching Ellie rush to her friend and confidant, at least the closest replica of a friend that Huet Pointe could provide. "May I get you two anything else for the moment?" Sabine asked.

"Not from that tray," Ernestine replied. "Those need to go in the trash now, being covered with her smut and all. Lord knows what she picks up in her line of work."

Happy to escape, Sabine wove through the crowd to the kitchen.

With flush cheeks and neck, Ellie found Bonnie entertaining Mr. Ferguson, her maternal grandmother, and several of Huet Pointe's elite in the parlor.

"'It is too full, oh the milk of human kindness to catch the nearest way.'" Bonnie giggled as she caught her breath and turned to Mr. Ferguson—blue eyes devouring blue eyes. "'Thou wouldst be great, art not without ambition,'" she recited. Then, with a wicked grin, "'But without the illness should attend it.'"

The small crowd applauded the performance, none prouder than Mr. Ferguson. "It seems my lovely Bonnie is both the beauty and the brains of this arrangement."

"Mother insisted I study Shakespeare," Bonnie said. "*Macbeth* is her favorite."

"Well, then, hopefully we can lure troupes to Mobile as well, or perhaps you will take over the humanities league and demand it." Soft, dark waves danced atop Mr. Ferguson's head as he gazed down at Bonnie.

"Well, Mister Ferguson, 'screw your courage to the sticking place and we'll not fail!'" Bonnie's laughter rose to a crescendo as her admirers looked on with slight confusion. "Just another line from the great William Shakespeare and his triumph *Macbeth*," Bonnie told them. She curtsied just as Ellie grabbed her arm.

"May I steal you away for a moment?" Ellie asked Bonnie. Then, the growing crowd, "This will just take a moment. A brief intermission if you will." Ellie plastered a smile across her face then tugged at Bonnie's arm, pulling her toward the porch.

"Ellie Weever, this better be good. Dragging me away like this," Bonnie said as Ellie backed her toward the porch railing. "What has lit your britches on fire?"

"Do you know anything about your mother trying to sell this place?"

"Pardon me?"

"Sell this house and the land and all that goes with it? Ernestine Harris is spreading a rumor around that your mother must sell or Mister Ferguson will call off the wedding. She just went on and on about your father's debt."

"Ernestine Harris is an old, cantankerous bag of bones whose life is too pathetic and boring to be paid a bit of mind."

"So, it's not true?"

Bonnie wind out over the front lawn. The breeze picked up one blonde tendril and bounced it off her chin.

"It's true?"

"Ellie, marriage is a complicated arrangement you know nothing about."

"I know matters of the heart. I know that your Mister Ferguson is not simply an *arrangement* to you. You would be devastated if he denied you. Just devastated."

"Ellie, did you bring me out here—against my will, mind you—to confirm what I already know? I'm the one who confided in you my fondness for Mister Ferguson. And I would appreciate you keeping my confidence. Mother would never forgive me if I allowed the Fergusons the upper hand."

"If your father's debt is true, so large that the estate and assets must be sold off and quickly, then they've already got the upper hand. Even an unengaged, unmarried woman such as myself knows that." Ellie glared at Bonnie, and for the first time saw Anna Beth's countenance in her face. "You should have told me."

"So you could what? Buy this place yourself? Painting up dead people can't be that profitable, Ellie. This is above your understanding and your means."

Bonnie's comment landed as a sucker punch.

"Your mother has taught you well," Ellie said. "Tell her that I will expect payment for Mister McLeary's preparations within the week. I don't have *the means* to allow it to slide any longer."

Stung, Bonnie wrapped the tendril back into a perfect cork-screw with one lithe finger. "Enjoy yourself tonight, Ellie," Bonnie said, and, "This will probably be the last gala in this dreadful town for some time."

Ellie watched Bonnie glide, no *float*, back into the house, swept up by yet another circle of admirers.

"Pardon me, excuse me," Ellie said, pushing her way past the whiskey-swilling Huet Pointe City Council, holding her breath through clouds of cigar smoke.

"That one's still available for your boy," one bloated elder said to another as Ellie squeezed by them, careful to avoid burning tips and wandering hands.

"His mother would never have her. She's pretty enough, but painting up dead bodies? No." The second elder caught Ellie's eye with his comment. A slight blush appeared on his cheeks.

Ellie fled to the back porch and into a near collision with Sabine. Her ankle tweaked against her boot at the abrupt stop. Ellie rotated her ankle, trying to coax the pain away.

"Oh, excuse me, Ma'am," Sabine said, catching the railing. "I was just enjoying the breeze. The air is getting thick inside."

"The air is thick out here, too."

"May I get you anything? Iced tea or a handkerchief?" Sabine motioned to the tear threatening to escape Ellie's eyes.

"Thank you. You're so kind. No, no. I don't need…You've always been kind to me, haven't you?"

"I try to be." Sabine glanced toward the door. "I should get back inside." As Sabine turned to go, Marguerite Alpuente Lawry, the recently fated Widow Lawry, rounded the corner of the wrap-around porch.

"Well, well, taking a little breather, are you?"

"Yes, the breeze is lovely, although it's picking up a bit out—"

"I wasn't speaking to you, Miss Weever." A bit of whiskey sloshed over the rim of Maggie's crystal highball glass. "You can leave," she told Ellie.

Ellie, preferring Bonnie's brand of snobbery to the terror Maggie Lawry could inflict, made a swift exit.

"Now," Maggie said turning to Sabine, "I didn't lend you out today so you could stare at the moon."

Sabine stared at the floor. "No, Ma'am. I just needed a little air before filling my tray…"

Maggie held up one hand, interrupting the much younger Sabine. "Have you asked forgiveness?"

"I was given permission to take a short break."

"Not for that, you twit. Have you asked forgiveness? Atoned for your sins?" Maggie's voice took on a venomous tone as she stepped closer to Sabine.

"I'm afraid I don't know what you are talking about." And she feared her only possible guess would be correct.

"Sure, you do. You know." Maggie took another step toward Sabine, closing the distance between them.

The sour combination of whiskey and crab bisque wafted into Sabine's nose. She felt the back of her throat clench.

"Don't worry. I won't tell," Maggie said, a sinister triviality displayed on her face.

"Please let me be," Sabine begged as Ray Don Lawry's face, mangled and cold, flashed in her mind. She squeezed her eyes shut trying to rid her skin of the remembrance but failed. Just like that, as if she was back in her shack rather than the McLearys' porch, Ray Don's hands gripped her shoulders and pressed her into the straw ticking of her bed.

"I know it was you." Maggie sipped from her glass, long and slow, gulping down the caramel brew.

"Please. I need to get back to work."

"'Things without all remedy should be without regard. What's done is done' and all that nonsense." Maggie brushed the tip of her nose against Sabine's cheek.

Maggie's glare chilled Sabine's soul so that in that moment, Sabine struggled to decipher who was Macbeth's wife, whose hands would never be washed clean: Lady Macbeth's, Marguerite Lawry's or her own.

"Look at me," Maggie mocked, "I'm precious Sabine. So pretty, so smart, so…so…You're no better than me. You're just a whore like the rest of us."

Sabine shook the fear from her face and made steel her expression. She was done with her mistress' cruelty as she had been done with Ray Don's weeks before. Only now, on the McLeary porch with the wind whipping up behind her, she had no pistol.

"No, I'm not," Sabine said. "Your husband used me as his whore, and I—"

"You what, my dear? Say it. Unburden your soul."

Sabine could feel the wooden railing digging into her back. She bent away from Maggie's stench; breath so hot it could peel the fancy wallpaper off the McLeary's walls. It was the smell that broke her last defenses. She choked on the smell and the memory flooded her every cell. Ray Don grunting. Ray Don's forearm against her throat, crushing her larynx. Thick, dirty fingers tearing at her undergarments.

Ray Don's mortal sin had lasted only one horrific minute, but in that minute, Sabine lost the peace her Dambalah, her Iwa, had given her. It shattered into fragments, spraying pieces on the mattress, the walls, the floor where Ray Don's gunbelt and pistol lay cocked from an interrupted then forgotten, drunken game of roulette. When Ray Don rose and stumbled to the open door, Sabine snatched the pistol from the floor.

"Perhaps I should promote you," Maggie said, pinning Sabine to the porch railing. "That was one hell of a shot."

Sabine banished the tears demanding her attention and pushed Maggie away. "It was luck. One awful, gruesome stroke of luck." Sabine then lifted her tray and walked through the servants' door leaving Maggie to fester on the porch—puss bubbling on a blister.

Inside, Sabine searched for Mamba Loo. A smile and kind word or even a smart remark would calm her, bring her back to the joy that was supposed to be that night in Huet Pointe. This was to be a night of art and culture and community, one Sabine would experience from the fringes, yes, and without her friend. Unknown to Sabine, Mamba Loo had abandoned her post and surrendered to the trees.

As darkness fell, every seat in the impressive McLeary dining room filled. The heavy, embroidered drapes were pulled tight to block the moonlight. Candles and oil lamps were lit along the apron and atop the mantle and swung from iron stands forming a proscenium for the makeshift stage. By the end of Act I, scene 1, nearly every Huet Pointe gentleman in his cravat and tails dozed, heads bobbing like buoys on the bayou. The women did not sleep. The women of Huet Pointe sat transfixed on one magnificent creature, the passionate and ruthless Lady Macbeth.

With hair as red as fire and flowing to her waist with soft curls only angels could have drawn, Lady Macbeth plotted. As she revealed her ambition cobalt blue eyes stared into the onlookers' souls. Muscular yet lovely hands reached out to choke what morality remained in Huet Pointe that night, as if to punctuate every deviant thought. Light bounced from lamp to pale skin and out to the audience, highlighting their own ambition, unjust successes, and certain failings.

"Make thick my blood," the actress recited toward the end of Act I. "Stop up the access and passage to remorse..."

Anna Beth glanced around the room from her chosen seat behind those she'd selected as potential buyers. "Make thick, indeed," she thought, "I will be the man Gil never was, never could be. I will rid Bonnie and me of this vulgar place and deliver the life we deserve." She smiled at Bonnie seated next to her and grasped her hand. Anna Beth's own mother glimpsed the supposed act of kindness and shared a grin—dawdling, displaced joy. "Simple-minded moron," Anna Beth thought, and returned her focus to the magnificent creature on stage.

Bonnie shifted in her seat, resting her head ever so lightly on her mother's shoulder and thanked God Almighty for the woman who gave her life. Anna Beth had crafted each moment of her courtship with Mr. Ferguson. Of that, Bonnie had no doubt, but had her mother rejected morality just as the homicidal redhead before? She examined the angle of her mother's chin, the sharp slope of her nose, the purse of her lips. "No, no," Bonnie thought, "Mother may lack the ability to feel guilt, but what has she to feel guilty of? Loving her daughter enough to do what must be done?" To Bonnie, anything short of murder would be worth her future with Mr. Ferguson. Her thoughts then were interrupted by whispering behind her.

"Would you two hush?" Bonnie whispered, twisting in her seat to glare at Rosarie and Ernestine, seated behind her and commenting on every detail as if theatre critics.

"You just mind your own," Ernestine replied, and turned again to the journal folded open in her lap.

"Did you get that last line? Woman's breasts and taking milk and something about murdering ministers?" Rosarie asked bent toward the page. She squinted at the chicken scratch, trying to make out words in the unsteady, dim light.

"Yes, yes, I got it if you will stop distracting me." Ernestine scribbled another line in her notebook—blind lettering from a nearly blind woman. "My Walter wants to know every detail of tonight. He'll be thrilled."

"Oh my goodness, is he speaking again?" Rosarie asked. The excitement of such a possibility betrayed her as her voice carried throughout the audience and bounced off the walls and ceiling.

Ernestine scowled at Rosarie, to her mind the epitome of helplessness and dumb optimism. "Don't be cruel." To Ernestine's dismay, companions were a meager crop in Huet Pointe—the fruit not always as ripe as one would like. Rosarie should have known as Ernestine did but never admitted fully that Walter Harris would never speak again.

Two rows further back, the evening had dissolved into a shroud of could-have-beens for Ellie Weever. The second-row seat she eyed during cocktail hour was indeed reserved for someone else. Ellie was shown to the last row furthest from the stage. Then, halfway through the first scene, Maggie Lawry had plopped herself into the chair right next to Ellie, dashing any remaining hope that the evening would prove enjoyable. But, it being the only chair left unoccupied, Ellie had no choice but to remain in Widow Lawry's cloud of whiskey and discontent through the first act. During intermission, with all her courage stuck to the whipping post, she'd thrown propriety to the whipping wind and attempted to steal someone else's seat during intermission. She'd never thought that Madam McLeary would prefer to sit directly behind Lulu Dann rather than her daughter's lifelong friend.

"Ellie, so wonderful of you to join us tonight. I see you're well," Anna Beth McLeary had said upon returning to her own seat nearing the end of intermission. "You should return to your seat now. The next act is about to begin. Four rows back, correct?" Anna Beth smoothed the satin of her skirt over her lap so that it ballooned around her like a shiny mushroom top.

"Correct," Ellie said. She eyed Bonnie, opening them so wide that her big, almond orbs begged for mercy. "I'll be going now," she told Bonnie. Bonnie nodded—one last plea for a pardon denied.

As the lights dimmed, three figures—male or female, who could tell—took the stage. They moved in haunting circles around a makeshift cauldron. Their dance continued as their volume grew and Maggie Lawry with glass refreshed swilled and spilled her way to her seat, late again. The brown drops from Maggie's glass formed wet dots on Ellie's satin skirt, turning into a sullied disaster. Ellie caught the sob creeping up in her throat just in time. No need to add further embarrassment to the evening.

"Eye of newt and toe of frog, wool of bat and tongue of dog, adder's fork and blind worm's sting," the shortest of the odd creatures chanted.

"Ha!" Maggie choked, "Sounds like my mother's gumbo!" She punctuated this outburst with an elbow to Ellie's ribcage.

With that, Ellie was done. She could take the evening no more. Ernestine and Rosarie and their gossip, Bonnie's rejection, her sore ankle still throbbing, Madam McLeary treating her with the indifference of a stranger not to mention Miz McLeary excluding any single man below the age of old fart from the guest list; each offense and transgression had eaten away at Ellie's composure. Now to be subjected to Maggie Lawry's uncouth behavior, which Ellie no doubt would be presumed guilty of due to her proximity to the insolent drunk, was too much for one woman to endure in a single evening. Like a mouse, Ellie rose from her seat, turned, and exited the dining room then the mansion. Few noticed her departure. Ellie assumed the angels intervened to quiet her skirts as she made her hasty retreat.

Ellie limped through the lavish gardens and past the dormant Angel's Trumpet. She'd wished they were in bloom. The luxurious fragrance lifted her spirits without fail, especially when reminded of her station, her inability to change it, and its accompanying, suffocating loneliness. But, on that night, no blooms opened to comfort her. In the darkness, only bubbling sulfur and hot wind pushed against her full skirt.

As Ellie passed the sugarcane fields, she saw Mamba Loo, seemingly frozen, her gaze fixed on the path through the stalks.

"Storm's coming," Mamba said, in a voice no louder than the flutter of a moth.

"Did you say something, Mamba?" Ellie asked.

"Better get on home now," Mamba said, "Storm's coming. Big one. Bad one."

Mamba Loo appeared as entranced as Shakespeare's witches. Her words chilled Ellie, even with the punishing humidity and June heat that felt more like mid-August.

"Perhaps you should, too," Ellie said, gazing at the tentacle clouds now swollen and charging toward their shared piece of sky. "You wouldn't want to get caught in whatever's coming."

Mamba Loo ignored Ellie's advice. That morning when the trees began their discord, Mamba suspected. When the blue skies turned to strips of grey, she feared. When the wind carried the trees' warning through the seams of the McLeary mansion, Mamba Loo knew. She knew what barreled toward Huet Pointe. It promised to be more of a reckoning than storm. Birnam Wood had indeed come to Dunsinane, charging forward as cavalry across a battle line. A storm like none other with winds capable of shredding oak trees, snapping the thickest vines, and pushing a wall of water twenty-five feet high into Huet Pointe.

Inside the McLeary Plantation home, heads and attention turned toward the howling wind. What was an hour before a growing breeze now rattled the windows. Without a word from Anna Beth, servants of all rank and size rushed the dining room. They shoved large armoires in front of the windows, scraping the polished floors. Chandeliers rocked to and fro as butlers attempted to extinguish the flames while others handed lanterns to the tuxedo-clad men in the audience, still seated, waiting for direction.

Lady Macbeth paused, staring at Anna Beth. The disruption was too great for her to continue.

Anna Beth stood and addressed the crowd. "We will take a brief," she said glaring at the butler nearest her, and "very brief pause while the servants ready the house. I'm sure the storm outside will pass quickly, but I would hate for any of you to be inconvenienced by a broken window or toppled flame. Remain seated, please. We will see the conclusion in just a moment." Satisfied, Anna Beth sat and fixed her gaze on the stage.

Sabine, ordered to extinguish candles in the parlor and other smaller rooms, searched frantically for Mamba Loo. It wasn't like Mamba to abandon her duty. She rushed out the back door and onto the porch. The wind, now punishing, tore at the Angel's Trumpet just beyond the porch railing. A green leaf slapped Sabine in the face as she trudged toward the railing, clutched it with one hand, and veiled her eyes with the other. Beyond the garden the trees danced—jerky, harried movements as if calling upon their own Iwa. Sabine trembled, for she knew where her dear Mamba Loo had gone.

Mamba Loo heard her fate in the trees. At the edge of the sugarcane fields, she marched ahead. She entered the tree line in silence. The silence grew deafening as she stopped at her favorite oak and bent to remove her shoes. Then, she unfurled her tignon. A faint smile crept across her face as the warm wind blew through her corkscrew tufts and onto her scalp. She fell to her knees. Prayed one Our Father and three Hail Marys. Thanked her Iwa and begged approval, forgiveness. Then she eased onto her backside and leaned against the tree. With her thick legs extended and bare toes, black with white pads, spread against the wind, she closed her eyes and listened to the water.

As the wind pushed the water on shore, tearing trees from their roots, overflowing shallow creeks, and flattening indiscriminately slave shack and colonial home alike, it declared what the Scottish queen never had a chance to that night, "Out, damn'd spot! Out, I say!" The water rose to form a black wall of atonement. For all the sins of Huet Pointe, it delivered fury and fear and horrid resolve.

❈

Epilogue

WHAT ELSE IS A WOMAN TO DO than speak her mind, admit her ambition, and try like hell to achieve it? The women of Huet Pointe beat their fists against the sliver of ground. They tore at the vines and cursed the rivers and creeks that swelled in the rain, turning their primitive streets into sinkholes. They fought the wind and breathed into lavender sachets when the wind shifted. They scrubbed the mold from windowsills and mildew from dark, humid corners. Again, what else could they do?

To all accounts, the Hurricane of 1851 arrived without warning. For thirteen punishing hours it violated Huet Pointe until nothing remained in way of defense. The water came and came. From the sea and sky, the land was soaked, overrun with water.

Few survived. Those who did live to tell the tale of that night did so floating upriver on scraps of rooftops. Families to the north of Huet Pointe took in what survivors they could, but soon grew weary of their descriptions of bloated, dead animals floating alongside them. Mothers shooed children from the room if mention of the water bursting into the McLeary dining room came up in conversation, then changed the subject before the more gruesome details were recounted.

Despite all the benefits of forgetting, those who survived could not forget the screams of the women as the water destroyed the windows and thrust every last one from their seats. Worse than the screams, however, was the gurgling. The water dragged woman and man alike from the home. Silk skirts became dead weight, made heavy with water. As if from below, the women were pulled under the surface. Flapping as they might, they could not fight the water. There, in a newly expanded bayou, the women perished, tangled in vines deep below the surface until nothing—not a ribbon, not a bauble, not even the boning in their corsets—remained.

Some would say Huet Pointe should have never been settled in the first place, that the land was too wild to tame. Many lamented that, if warned, the town could have been saved. But warnings are often ignored. Some would share the story turned legend of Huet Pointe from pulpits and soapboxes. "Let these poor souls be a reminder of God's vengeance!"

No matter who was right and who was wrong, one truth could not be denied: The storm washed Huet Pointe clean.

Book Club Questions

1. Mamba Loo makes herself ugly to achieve her goals. How do we today change or alter ourselves to achieve our goals? Does modern society pressure women in particular to change themselves to achieve their goals? Can women be outwardly ambitious or does ambition in women carry stigmas?

2. Maggie and Ray Don must have loved each other at some point in their relationship, but that love eroded over the years. Is Maggie Lawry justified in her actions against Ray Don and their marriage? If so, why? Is Maggie—after all she has done—redeemable?

3. Sabine leans on her faith to ease her struggle in the world, as many do today. Do you believe Sabine uses her faith and religious practices for protection from reality, escape from reality, or both? If so, how does she do this?

4. Do you as a reader sympathize with Ernestine? Is she justified in her behavior towards Ellie Weaver? Contrast Ernestine's actions against Ellie Weaver and her actions to aid her friend Rosalie. How can both these acts—supposedly killing a dog and protecting an abused friend—be committed by the same person?

5. Is Anna McLeary an example of greed and selfishness, or an example of a woman trapped in a social construct in which she

has little to no control over her life? Is her financial predicament after Mr. McLeary's death justice for her bad deeds?

6. Lulu has achieved her professional goals, but still battles
personal demons. What is preventing her from living happily,
satisfied with her station in life?

7. Why does Mamba Loo sacrifice herself to the storm?

8. Which character, if any, do you sympathize with in Huet
Pointe? Which character, if any, did you wish would fail in
her ambition? What makes you root for failure or success for
each woman of Huet Pointe?

About the Author

JODIE CAIN SMITH is a graduate of the University of South Alabama and Northern Michigan University because earning a degree on both the southern and northern border happened by pure chance and a bit of study. She is the author of *The Woods at Barlow Bend*, her debut novel based on the true story of her grandmother's tumultuous adolescence in rural Alabama. Her short works have appeared in *The Petigru Review*, *Pieces Anthology*, and *Chicken Soup for the Military Spouse's Soul*. When not creating fictional worlds on her laptop, Jodie hangs out with her long-suffering husband and the most precious boy ever created. Seriously, the kid is amazing, and the husband puts up with a lot.